# SECRET SHORES

## LANTERN BEACH EXPOSURE
## BOOK 6

## CHRISTY BARRITT

# ALSO BY CHRISTY BARRITT

Find a full list of Christy Barritt's books at: www.christybarritt.com.

# CHAPTER
# ONE

RACHEL ATWOOD STOOD on the Lantern Beach boardwalk and gazed toward the Atlantic Ocean.

If only the scene brought her peace. Usually, it did.

But today, police surrounded a man and woman on the beach.

The couple had their beach chairs raised over their heads, using them as weapons. Though they targeted each other, innocent beachgoers around them were also in the line of fire.

Three police officers currently attempted to apprehend the duo.

Rachel had never seen anything like it.

She'd stumbled upon the scene as she walked, attempting to enjoy the beautiful Saturday in August.

As she stood there watching, her phone buzzed.

She glanced at the screen and recognized the number. This caller had tried to reach her yesterday also. But so much static had filled the line that whatever this person had been trying to tell her hadn't been understandable. Rachel only knew that the voice on the other line had sounded desperate . . . almost panicked.

Tension knotted her muscles as she put the phone to her ear. "Hello?"

"Rachel . . ." a female said on the other line. "I . . . need . . ."

"Who is this?" She gripped the phone more tightly.

"Experimenting . . ."

Experimenting? What could that mean?

She turned away from the chaos on the beach to give the conversation her full attention. "I'm sorry, but I couldn't hear you. You said something about experimenting?"

"Need . . . your help . . . no one else."

No one else what? No one else could help?

Shouts sounded from the beach and distracted her. She craned her neck to watch the commotion again.

Two officers had managed to grab the man and the third officer went after the woman, who'd tackled another man who'd been nearby before running away.

Drugs? Most likely.

"Ocean . . . Essence . . ." the caller said.

Rachel's blood went cold, and all her attention snapped back to the caller.

Wait . . . someone needed help because Ocean Essence was running experiments?

That didn't make sense. Sure, the company did clinical trials. But those were all conducted in a safe laboratory environment.

There was no reason someone should call wanting Rachel's help.

Whoever was on the other line was clearly distressed—especially since she'd called twice.

But why was this woman calling her? Because Rachel worked as a scientist at Ocean Essence?

"I'm not sure what you want me to do," Rachel said. "Where are you located? Isn't there a clinical trial organizer who might be able to help you?"

"Not . . . official. Against . . . will."

Rachel's heart began to beat overtime.

If she understood this conversation correctly, the company she worked for was experimenting on people without their permission. How could that even be the case? She didn't want to believe it was true.

"Where are you?" Rachel rushed.

But before the caller could answer, someone grabbed Rachel's arm.

Something hard and pointy pressed into her back until she let out a gasp.

She glanced over her shoulder—just barely—and saw a man wearing a baseball cap and sunglasses. He stood beside her but didn't look at her.

At once, she knew the object pressing into her back was a gun.

Suddenly, her phone call was forgotten.

"What are you doing?" She lowered the phone, shoving it back into her pocket.

"Don't ask questions. You just need to walk." The man's voice sounded gruff and unyielding as he propelled her forward.

She instantly knew she couldn't go anywhere with this man.

She had a better chance of surviving out in the open than she did anywhere this guy might take her.

That meant she needed to think fast.

What would Jonah do?

His image sprang to her mind.

The two had dated for several months before Jonah had abruptly called things off and moved off the island. She hadn't heard from him since.

Rachel was still heartbroken and tried not to think about him.

But she did. Too often.

She should have known better than to give her heart to any man. She'd learned that lesson before meeting Jonah, but she'd quickly forgotten it.

Jonah was a skilled operative—first with the military and now with the Shadow Agency. He seemed to know how to get out of every dangerous situation.

She needed to think like he would right now.

"Just keep walking," the man grumbled. "Don't give any indication you have a gun to your back or I *will* pull this trigger." As if to drive home his point, the man shoved the gun harder into her ribcage.

Rachel let out another gasp.

Tourists milled around the boardwalk, oblivious of the armed man beside her as they shopped for beach accessories or souvenirs to take home. Some ate popcorn, and others had cotton candy or soft pretzels.

The festive atmosphere was usually so uplifting.

As if people had no clue that two people in bathing suits were trying to whack each other with beach chairs on the other side of the shops.

Or that a stranger held a gun to Rachel's back.

*Keep thinking, Rachel. You can't go with him.*

Her gaze darted around as she tried to figure out her plan of escape.

Children mingled in the crowd. If Rachel made a wrong move, they could be put in danger. She could never live with herself if something happened to one of them because of her.

"Keep going," the gunman said through what sounded like gritted teeth.

They were headed toward the parking lot, she realized.

Rachel couldn't get into a vehicle with him. She'd be a goner.

What happened in the next few minutes could mean life or death.

*Her* life or death.

She tried to steal another glance at the gunman, to see if she recognized him.

But the man seemed nondescript, unfamiliar, not like anyone she'd seen before.

Why in the world would he want to take her away at gunpoint? Because of the kind of scientific work she did, certainly she could be targeted by someone who might want to use her skills for nefarious reasons. But she didn't exactly go around announcing she had earned two PhDs.

Ahead, she spotted her friend's ice cream truck parked close to the boardwalk. A long line of people waited to get their sweet treats from Serena.

Maybe this was Rachel's chance to escape. The line wound across the boardwalk like a serpent. The congestion made this area harder to maneuver.

And presented an opportunity.

"Good girl," the man muttered. "Keep going. Look casual. Or else."

They made their way through the crowd unnoticed. Rachel was still keenly aware of the gun jabbing into her. One reaction, one jerk of the finger . . . and it would all be over for her.

As soon as she passed through the mob, she would act.

Two more steps.

And . . . now!

She stopped suddenly and swung her leg toward the back of the man's knees. He wobbled, grabbing onto a nearby woman to keep from falling.

The tourist screamed.

The crowd began to scatter. Some gasped. Others pulled out their cell phones to take pictures.

Rachel wasted no time. She sprinted in the opposite direction.

She had to get away.

Her gaze scanned everyone around her as she looked for a familiar face who might be able to help.

She saw only tourists.

Making a last-minute decision—one that she hoped she didn't regret—she darted inside Beach Bound Books and Beans.

Her friend Tali MacArthur owned this place, and she was also married to the town's former police chief.

As soon as Rachel ran inside, she locked the door behind her.

Tali's eyes widened, and she crossed from around the coffee bar to meet her. "Rachel . . . are you okay?"

Rachel glanced out the window, desperate to see if she'd been followed.

But no one was behind her.

However, that didn't mean the man was gone.

"Rachel?" Tali repeated as she stared at Rachel with concern in her eyes.

Rachel shook her head. "A man . . . he's chasing me . . . with a gun."

As she said the words, Rachel realized she had something in common with the woman who'd called her only moments before.

They both sounded scared and desperate.

If Rachel got out of this current situation alive, she planned to figure out exactly who had called her and why.

———

From behind the tinted glass of his SUV, Jonah Gray stared at the apartment building nestled on the outskirts of Chicago.

Surveillance wasn't nearly as fun or glamorous as they made it look on TV.

In fact, it was one of the least favorite parts of his job with the Shadow Agency.

But he knew the risks of his current assignment.

They were high. Too high.

The implications extended beyond just him.

If they didn't get this assignment right, thousands of innocent people might suffer.

Jonah couldn't let that happen.

Instead, he and his team had to muddle through the mundane details of the case in order to get these criminals off the street.

Gage Pearson, his colleague, sat beside him and stared out the window with the same glazed look in his eyes.

Three hours down. Six more to go.

At least they could listen to Tim McGraw on the radio. It was something to help pass the time.

Just then, Jonah's phone rang.

A name he didn't expect to see popped up on his screen.

Roman Atwood.

Why in the world would he be calling? The last time they'd spoken . . . Roman hadn't been happy with Jonah. Rightfully so.

The last thing Jonah had wanted was to hurt Roman's daughter, Rachel. He should have called things off earlier. Before they were both in too deep. Before things became even more complicated.

But he'd been sucked into a fantasy where he thought happily ever after might actually exist.

Then Jonah's friend had almost been killed and was currently in ICU.

A hit had been put out on him and his team members.

And Jonah had known that anyone he cared about could be in danger.

"Are you going to get that?" Gage nodded at Jonah's phone.

"I'll just be a minute." He hit Accept, and then put the phone to his ear.

But he kept his gaze on that apartment building just in case their target emerged. Jonah couldn't allow himself to get distracted.

Which was why answering this call was so risky.

"Mr. Atwood." Tension stretched across Jonah's chest, even though he tried to make his voice sound casual. "How's it going?"

"Not good." Roman's voice cracked. "It's Rachel."

Jonah's heart lodged in his throat, and his current mission faded to the back of his mind. "What's going on?"

He'd left Lantern Beach to keep her safe. So what could have happened? Did she have some type of medical emergency? An accident?

"A man pulled a gun on her today, and he tried to force her into his car."

"What?" Alarm raced through him, and he straightened. "Is Rachel okay?"

"She managed to get away. She's shaken but fine."

"Do you know who did this?" His thoughts suddenly rapid fired and his boredom was forgotten.

"As of right now, no. The police have no idea. But I'm worried about her. She was on the boardwalk when he approached her. That man didn't randomly pick her from the crowd. He targeted her. And I fear he'll target her again and again until he gets what he wants . . . whatever that is." Roman's voice cracked.

Jonah's thoughts whirred. He had a lot of enemies. What if one of them found out about Rachel and the fact he had feelings for her?

Amar Ravish was the reason he'd left Lantern Beach. The terrorist was brutal and bent on revenge. But other terrorist organizations would also love to bring Jonah down—and hurt those he loved in the process.

Some of those men might want to retaliate against Jonah by going after Rachel—the exact scenario he'd desperately tried to avoid.

Nausea pooled inside him at the thought.

"She would never call and tell you this herself," Roman continued. "But I'm not willing to leave this to chance."

Jonah could read between the lines and knew what Roman was saying without actually saying it.

"I'll hop on the next plane and get back to Lantern Beach."

"I was hoping you'd say that." Audible relief rang through Roman's voice.

"But Rachel may not want to see me," Jonah reminded Roman.

"Her safety is more important than her feelings. It's not normally something I'd say, but I think you're the only one who can help her. I know things didn't end well . . . you're not my favorite person right now. But I know you're capable."

A plan had already formed in Jonah's mind. A plan that involved keeping Rachel safe, even if it was under lock and key.

Maybe not that extreme.

But he'd do whatever it took to make sure no one hurt her. He wouldn't trust anyone else with the task.

He ended the call and turned to Gage. "I'm going to need someone to replace me."

Gage raised his eyebrows. "What do you think Larchmont is going to say about that?"

Larchmont was their boss and someone people didn't cross.

"Right now . . . I don't care what he says. The woman I love is in danger, and I need to protect her."

# CHAPTER
# TWO

RACHEL WAS STILL SHAKEN that night as she sat curled on the couch remembering what had happened.

She'd called the police, of course. By the time they'd arrived, the gunman was long gone.

Officers had interviewed witnesses, but no one could really describe this guy other than to say he was of medium height with a medium build and that he wore a baseball cap and sunglasses.

She had no hopes that anyone would be able to track him down.

The thought terrified her.

That guy had clearly wanted something from her. Since he hadn't gotten whatever that was today, she felt certain he'd be back to finish what he had started.

Rachel had gone home after talking to the police

and had vowed to stay inside for the rest of the day. It was Saturday anyway, and she had nothing else scheduled.

Not anymore.

Not since Jonah had left a month ago.

Her heart still panged with regret when she thought about him. Thought about how wrong she'd been to trust him with her heart.

But at least her dad was back now. He was safe after a harrowing experience several months ago.

At this moment, Dad was in his office working on another invention. He'd made a name for himself after creating household cleaning gadgets that did the work for you—such as robots that mopped the floor and even a machine that cleaned windows.

Rachel had insisted that he prepare for an upcoming meeting and not dote over her. His doting only made her more nervous.

But as her gaze hit the Scrabble board sitting on her coffee table near the fireplace, another pang of regret filled her.

Some of her favorite memories of her time with Jonah involved the two of them playing Scrabble at night while drinking hot tea.

She should have known their time together wouldn't last. It was simply too good to be true.

A noise cut through the memory, startling her until she nearly spilled her tea.

Someone rang the doorbell.

Who had come by? Maybe the police were following up about the earlier incident.

The doorbell sounded again.

Caution pinched her spine as she crept toward the entrance.

She peered out the peephole just to be safe.

Rachel sucked in a breath when she saw the person on the other side.

Jonah Gray.

He was back. In Lantern Beach. Standing outside her oceanfront house.

Why would he be here . . . ?

She reached for the door but hesitated. Maybe she should pretend like she didn't hear the doorbell. Maybe he'd think no one was home, and he'd go away. That way, she wouldn't have to talk to him.

But that wasn't the way she operated.

Avoiding problems never made them better. It only delayed the inevitable.

She might as well get this conversation over with.

Tension pulled taut through her muscles as she jerked the door open. She didn't even give Jonah a chance to say anything. Instead, she blurted, "What are you doing here?"

He leaned against the side of the house, his legs crossed, his hands in his pockets, and that rakish look in his eyes that Rachel had thought was so attractive at one time.

The porch light illuminated his blond hair as it swept over his forehead in a stylishly messy way, and his gray jeans and blue shirt showed off his fit physique.

Okay, she still thought he was handsome. But she didn't *want* to think that. She wanted to forget him and all the feelings he stirred inside her.

"Rachel . . . it's been a while." His voice sounded surprisingly gentle.

She couldn't fall under his spell again. She was the one who'd ended up as a frog. "I said, what are you doing here?"

"Can we talk inside?" He nodded behind her as he straightened, suddenly not appearing as casual. "It would be safer."

"Safer? Wait . . . did my dad call you?" Her dad had been a flurry of worry when Rachel told him about the incident at the boardwalk. But an hour later, he seemed unreasonably calm.

It was because he had a plan, wasn't it? He'd called Jonah.

"I should've known." Rachel started to shut the door, desperate to pretend none of this had happened. She was so tired of drama and chaos.

Jonah held up a hand. "Can you at least listen? Please?"

She hesitated as she studied his face and thought she saw sincerity there.

Then again, she'd fallen for that sincerity before.

What should she do? Hear him out? Or make it clear that she never wanted to talk to him again?

That was the choice she needed to make right now.

And with her heart on the line . . . everything felt entirely more complicated than it should.

———

Based on the fire in Rachel's eyes, convincing her to let him help was going to be harder than Jonah anticipated.

She had every reason to be upset with him.

However, right now, he needed to convince her to listen. Not for his sake, but for hers.

Based on the hardness of her jaw, that would be easier said than done.

She started to shut the door again.

He jutted his foot out to stop it—a tactic he hated to use. But she'd left him no choice. Jonah had to convince her to let him protect her.

"Rachel . . . please." He begged her with his gaze. "I know what happened earlier. You're not safe."

She studied him but didn't deny the truth in his words.

He waited, giving her time to process the conversation.

He knew she liked to think things through. She was a scientist, someone who loved logic and reasoning. He needed to respect that now.

"How do you think you can help keep me safe?" she finally asked, her voice disturbingly gentle.

"I can be a second set of eyes."

She still didn't soften. "I thought you had a more important job to do where you couldn't be here in Lantern Beach."

Ouch. But he deserved her pointed tone. "When I heard you were in danger, I gave that assignment up. I knew I needed to come back here instead."

What appeared to be a small flicker of a truce flashed through her gaze. But Jonah knew he'd need a lot more than that before she let him in again.

He lowered his voice. "It's not safe for us to talk out here. Not until I know more."

She let out a sigh but didn't otherwise move for several seconds.

Finally, she stepped back and opened the door wide. "Fine. Come in. But I can't promise you you're going to be welcome inside this house for long."

He nodded, relief filling him. At least he'd made it past the first obstacle.

But he still had a lot of work to do before he reached the finish line.

Now he needed more information. Maybe Rachel wouldn't let him into her life emotionally. But even if she'd share a little about what was going on right now . . . maybe he could pinpoint who was behind the earlier incident.

Did this ping back to Jonah and his enemies? Or did this have something to do with her work at Ocean Essence?

That was what he needed to figure out. He would need Rachel's help to do so.

He stepped inside the familiar two-story house, one raised on stilts like most of the homes in the area.

At once, memories filled him.

Some of the happiest times of his entire life had occurred between these walls.

Because this was where he'd fallen in love with Rachel. It was where they'd shared parts of their lives and opened up to each other.

As a kid who'd grown up in the foster care system, it wasn't often he'd felt such acceptance and understanding.

But Rachel had been different. She'd felt like forever.

That was why it had been so hard to leave her. But it had been for her own good.

She led him into the kitchen, her walk stiff.

She nodded to the table, not bothering to offer him a drink.

Jonah wasn't offended. Manners were the last thing on his mind right now.

They both sat down across from each other.

There was so much he wanted to say. But those conversations would have to wait until later.

Right now, they had more urgent matters to discuss.

# CHAPTER
## THREE

RACHEL COULDN'T BELIEVE Jonah was here in Lantern Beach.

Again.

She thought he'd walked out of her life permanently.

Yet here he was. Sitting across from her. Looking as handsome as ever.

And his concern . . . well, she wished she couldn't sense it. Its presence made her wonder if he still cared.

And wondering those things was dangerous.

She resisted a frown, not wanting to give Jonah the satisfaction of knowing how much he'd hurt her.

Satisfaction? Was that really how Rachel thought he felt?

She had trouble believing he felt any delight in

breaking her heart. In her worst moments, he'd been the ultimate jerk. In her best moments, she'd thought maybe there had been regret in his eyes.

But never satisfaction or smugness.

He wasn't that type of person.

This was all thanks to her dad. He clearly had something to do with Jonah's presence here.

It was the only reason he hadn't come out of his room when the doorbell rang twice. He was probably feigning not hearing the sound so he could give Rachel and Jonah some privacy.

She wasn't sure who'd been more heartbroken after their breakup: Rachel or her father. Her dad had adored Jonah. And why wouldn't he? Jonah had fit right in and become the son her father never had.

She'd have to have a talk with Dad later.

Jonah stared at her, an earnest look in his eyes. "Can you tell me what happened today?"

Rachel swallowed hard as the events from earlier that day flashed back into her mind.

She wished she could forget. That she could pretend the incident hadn't happened.

But it had.

After a deep breath, she ran through the details of being on the boardwalk. Of someone sneaking up behind her. Of feeling the gun pressed into her back.

Should she include the phone call? The people acting crazy on the beach?

She didn't think those things were connected . . . because that seemed unlikely. Right?

Jonah's gaze darkened with each new piece of information. "And you have no idea who that guy was?"

"I didn't get a good look at his face, but he didn't sound even vaguely familiar to me."

"Is there any reason why someone would want to do that to you? Anything I've missed since I've been gone?"

Since he'd been gone? Jonah had said the words as if he'd simply been on a business trip and planned on returning.

No, when he'd left the island, it had been permanent. He'd moved on . . . without Rachel.

She swallowed her emotions, knowing they would only complicate the situation right now. "Your guess is as good as mine. I haven't made any enemies lately if that's what you're asking."

A fleeting look passed through his gaze.

Rachel stiffened. He knew something he wasn't telling her, didn't he?

She could press him, but she felt certain he wouldn't answer. The details about his job were so secretive. She knew he worked classified assignments. But that part of his life had been totally closed to her, a chapter she wasn't allowed to access.

"I'm not sure what you think you can accomplish

by being here." Rachel knew her tone might be harsh, but she spoke the truth.

Jonah's gaze locked with hers. "I want to keep you safe."

But what was safe? That question had been on her mind for a long time.

Was there even such a thing as safe? Living required risk. To eliminate all risk . . . well, it meant not living life to the fullest—or anywhere close to it, for that matter.

She shifted on the couch as she considered how to respond.

Before she could, Jonah spoke again.

"I can keep an eye on you in case something like this happens again." Jonah's voice sounded confident as if he'd thought this through.

"And how long do you plan on sticking around?" Rachel's voice cracked with emotion. "Because for all I know, I could be in danger for the rest of my life. I know you can't stay that long. So why delay the inevitable? I'm going to need to learn to fend for myself. I can't always rely on my ex-boyfriend for help."

Yes, her words were pointed. But what she'd said was the stark truth.

She needed space. Having Jonah show back up in her life again may make things easier for a short time. But in the long run, his presence would only make things more difficult.

Before they could talk anymore, a thump sounded from somewhere inside the house.

Rachel rushed to her feet as alarm raced through her. Was the gunman back? Had she been so hyper-focused on this conversation that she'd let her guard down?

"My dad . . ." she muttered.

What if someone had broken in and hurt her father?

She raced toward his office, praying he was okay.

———

Jonah heard the thump and jumped to his feet.

Even though Rachel took off before he did, he managed to push himself in front of her.

No way was she running into a dangerous situation first. Not if he could help it.

"Where is your dad?" he called.

"In his office."

He headed toward the room and threw the door open.

He immediately saw the open window. Felt the humid air.

His gaze shifted to the floor.

Roman lay there, blood on his forehead.

Rachel let out a cry as she hurried to her father's side. She knelt on the floor and grabbed his arms. "Dad . . . are you okay?"

He blinked and tried to sit up, but his eyes appeared dazed. "I'm . . . fine."

Jonah raced to the window and peered out.

The darkness stared back.

Whoever had done this was gone.

Maybe.

"Stay with him," Jonah rushed. "And call the police."

Wasting no time, he climbed out the window and landed with a thump on the deck lining the back of the house.

He glanced around, his muscles taut.

He still saw no one.

Making a quick decision, Jonah headed to the right. There were fewer houses that way.

His feet dug into the sand as he took off down the shore.

But after a couple of blocks, he paused and scanned the area.

Whoever that man had been, he was gone now. He'd clearly had a getaway plan.

Still on guard, Jonah made his way back to the house.

He hoped Rachel had called the police as he'd asked.

Now he needed to make sure her dad was okay.

He went to the front door and twisted the handle. It was locked.

Good.

Instead, he rang the doorbell. "Rachel. It's me. Jonah."

A moment later, she answered. The worried look remained in her eyes, and lines of concern stretched across her forehead. "Anything?"

He shook his head, almost disappointed with himself and his answer. "Nothing."

Her frown deepened, and she motioned for him to follow her back inside.

As he did, Jonah made sure the door locked behind them.

Roman sat on the couch, a wet cloth to his forehead.

He looked disheveled but otherwise okay.

Jonah paused in front of him and sat on the edge of the sturdy coffee table. "How are you?"

"I'm still alive," he murmured, his wry humor emerging.

"What happened?" Jonah continued.

"I was sitting there working on one of my projects when I heard a noise. By the time I looked over, I saw the window had been shoved open. A man wearing black climbed inside. I stood, about to run and call for help. Before I could, the man grabbed me and threw me to the floor."

Jonah and Rachel exchanged a look.

If there was any doubt this danger would continue, with this new attack the uncertainty dissipated faster than dew on a hot day. Whoever it was must have realized Rachel wasn't here alone and fled.

This person—possibly one of Amar's men—wanted Rachel for some reason and would go to desperate measures to abduct her. Jonah didn't know what this person planned to do after that.

He knew all about the danger that had infiltrated everyday life here in the US. He knew about the danger most people were oblivious to—as they should be.

As part of his job, he learned about new threats every day. He took the bad guys down, sometimes even before the government realized what was going on.

His assignments were usually off book. They were hired by the rich and powerful. The company he worked for didn't officially exist.

But Jonah had made a promise to himself never to do a job that compromised his integrity.

Before they could talk anymore, sirens sounded outside the house.

"Cassidy must be here." Rachel rose.

Cassidy Chambers was the police chief on the island, and someone Rachel considered a friend. They were close to the same age and were members of the same church. Plus, Rachel had grown up spending summers here as a child, and one of her old friends was Ty Chambers, Cassidy's husband.

As Rachel stepped toward the door to let her inside, Jonah remained with Roman.

The two men exchanged a look that took the place of an hour-long conversation.

They were both worried about Rachel.

And Jonah knew without a doubt that coming to Lantern Beach had been the right choice.

# CHAPTER
# FOUR

AN HOUR LATER, Cassidy left.

She'd taken their statements and sent two officers out to look for the man. They hadn't found him. Another officer had searched the office for any clues the intruder may have left but found nothing.

While there, Cassidy had asked Rachel the question everyone else had on their minds. *Do you know who might be responsible for this?*

Rachel's answer remained the same. *I have no idea.*

Once Cassidy left, awkward silence fell between Jonah and Rachel as they stood in the living room.

Her father, after being cleared by paramedics, had excused himself to lie down. He was supposed to go on a trip early tomorrow morning and meet with a large company about a new product he was developing.

Given everything that had happened, he'd offered to stay in town, but Rachel had told him he should go. She couldn't let him miss this opportunity. He'd still looked uncertain, but he had promised to go to bed early, just in case.

As Rachel and Jonah stood there a moment, awkward silence falling between them, her phone buzzed. She glanced at the screen and saw a text from her friend and colleague Noelle Purdy. They'd talked about getting coffee together this week.

As soon as Rachel felt her phone buzz, it brought back memories of that earlier call. Even if other events had superseded it, the call had still been frightening.

"What is it?" Jonah's voice cut into her memories.

Rachel quickly shoved her phone back into her pocket. "What do you mean?"

He narrowed his eyes, clearly seeing right through her. "You frowned when your phone buzzed. Why?"

She considered a moment whether or not she should share about the phone call. Although it was odd, Rachel had no evidence anything was wrong—only assumptions and theories. For all she knew, the call was a misunderstanding or a joke.

She didn't think so, however.

Did that broken conversation have anything to do with the gunman?

Rachel had trouble believing that might be the case.

Then again . . . it very well could. As of right now, they had no answers. No motive. No anything.

Because of that, even the details that seemed the most inconsequential could be important.

Rachel stared Jonah down another moment as she contemplated how to respond to his inquiry. *You frowned when your phone buzzed. Why?*

How much should she tell him?

Even more important—how much did she want to let him in?

———

Jonah waited, hoping he wouldn't have to prod any more.

He wanted to give Rachel space. But he also knew she wasn't telling him something. He'd spent enough time with her to recognize her hesitation meant something was up.

After a moment of contemplation, she finally sighed and shifted her weight from one foot to the other. "Don't read too much into this, but I've gotten two strange phone calls recently from the same number."

The muscles in his back tightened faster than a

spring-loaded mousetrap. "What kind of phone calls?"

She shrugged, looking as if she wanted to appear casual. But Jonah saw the tension simmering in her gaze.

"The first call was staticky, and the caller's voice kept cutting in and out," Rachel said. "Honestly, I couldn't make out anything the person said. I thought it was a woman, but I couldn't even be sure of that. I didn't really think much of it. Maybe it was the wrong number or spam."

Jonah studied her face—her beautiful face, complete with wide eyes, full lips, and even features. Her dark brown hair fell over her shoulders, and her alabaster skin she kept protected from the sun because of her vitiligo. The skin condition caused some discoloration, but Rachel was working to find a solution to help others with the disease.

He could stare at her all day if he had the opportunity.

And Rachel's permission.

But he'd messed that up. He'd broken her heart in a way that might mean ever repairing things between them would be impossible.

"You didn't recognize the number?" He tried to clear his thoughts. Thinking about the past would do him no good right now.

Rachel shook her head. "I didn't. It was an out of state area code that I'm not familiar with."

"And then?"

"Then today, right before the man with the gun grabbed me . . ." She paused as she took in a shaky breath. "I got a phone call again from the same number. I answered, and the connection was pretty much the same. Except this time I could make out a few words, at least."

"What did the caller say?"

"It was definitely a woman. From what I could make out, she said something about needing help and Ocean Essence."

Jonah crossed his arms, not liking the sound of this. He'd been suspicious about the company for a long time—perhaps rightfully so. "You have no idea what that means?"

"No idea."

"Did this person use your name?"

Rachel's skin dropped a couple of shades. Then she pushed a dark lock of hair behind her ear and nodded. "She did. Oh, and she mentioned something about experimenting on people without permission."

"Experimenting?" At once, Jonah's thoughts raced back to his time in the military.

He'd been subjected to experiments after being recruited for a top-secret mission during his time in the Navy. Back then, he hadn't realized the project he'd been handpicked for involved scientists and injections and covert missions.

He still had scars from everything he'd been through—and more enemies than he could count.

He'd felt like a lab rat. The feeling wasn't something he'd ever wish on anyone.

The fact that Rachel worked for that cosmetics company only increased his worry. He'd suspected for a while that something nefarious was going on behind the scenes at Ocean Essence.

Someone at the company had murdered Jonah's friend. That person was now behind bars.

But Jonah still suspected something else was going on.

"What are you thinking?" Rachel stared up at him, unable to hide her shivers.

More than anything, Jonah wished he could wrap his arms around her and offer some comfort.

But he couldn't.

He swallowed hard at the thought.

"I haven't put anything together yet. But I don't like the sound of this." He rubbed his jaw, trying to measure both his words and his emotions.

She shrugged. "Like I said, it could just be nothing."

"Or it could be everything."

Rachel pressed her lips together and didn't argue. How could she?

She was reasonable. She had to know what he'd said was true.

"Can you send me the phone number the caller used?" Jonah implored her with his gaze, praying she didn't dig her heels in on this issue. That would only make everything harder. "I'll follow up. See if I can find out where the call originated from."

"I can do that." Rachel pulled out her phone and tapped her fingers on the screen. "Okay. I just texted it to you."

Jonah's phone buzzed in his pocket. "Thanks. I'll look into it."

They stood there a moment as more awkward silence filled the space between them.

He hated that their relationship had come down to this.

Then he reminded himself his decisions had all been for Rachel's sake.

It was best if the two of them kept their distance from each other.

But in the process, both of their hearts just might break again. However, he could deal with a broken heart more easily than he could handle Rachel being hurt . . . or killed.

RACHEL HATED the feeling swirling in her gut right now.

It had nothing to do with the gunman today or even the mysterious phone call she'd received.

It had *everything* to do with the fact that Jonah was standing in front of her.

She wasn't sure what kind of deal he and her father had discussed. Was her dad expecting Jonah to stay here? With his late arrival on the island, was there even anywhere else he could stay on Lantern Beach? Accommodations quickly filled to capacity in the summer.

When she remembered how Jonah had broken her heart, her resolve to keep her distance hardened.

Having him stay in her house would feel entirely too strange, too awkward. He should find somewhere else for the night. His sleeping arrangements weren't her problem.

Rachel drew in a deep breath before saying, "Thank you for coming out. I know Dad asked you to. But you being here isn't really necessary."

"Rachel—"

She raised her hand in a stop position. "No, really. I can handle this. Cassidy knows everything that's happening now, and she should be able to catch this guy. I know you have very important work to do."

She caught herself overly emphasizing the words "very important work" and frowned. The edge to her voice was born of hurt. But she could be an adult about this.

Jonah stared at her another moment, those blue eyes imploring hers.

Finally, he took a step back as if reluctantly accepting her decision. "I don't want to impose."

"It's probably better that you don't." Her throat burned at the statement. The truth was, she'd feel safer—physically—if he were here. But emotionally? His presence would expose all the tender parts of her.

He nodded slowly, almost resolutely. "If it's okay, I'll check in again tomorrow."

Rachel shrugged, not giving him a yes or a no.

Jonah's gaze lingered on her yet another moment as if there were things he wanted to say.

But he didn't. Whatever was on his mind, he kept those thoughts to himself.

Finally, he nodded. "Okay, I'll give you a call in the morning."

Regret instantly filled her.

But why?

Why was there a part of her that wanted to beg Jonah to stay?

Feelings were so tricky. Rachel would take science any day over emotions. At least with science, you dealt with facts. Absolutes. Data.

With emotions . . . well, nothing seemed certain or could be proven. Feelings fluctuated too much.

If Rachel had kept her heart closed, she could have avoided a lot of agony.

Jonah grabbed the doorknob and twisted it.

But when he opened it, a man stood on the deck outside her front door.

Even in the darkness, Rachel saw his dilated pupils. The foam at his mouth.

He almost looked . . . rabid.

But mostly what she noticed was the beach umbrella in his hands.

One he held like a javelin as he started to charge at Jonah.

———

Jonah's adrenaline surged when he saw the man standing there waiting to attack.

"Get back!" Jonah shoved Rachel behind him just as the man charged them.

Jonah ducked low, keeping his shoulder out.

He hit the man's abdomen.

The action propelled the guy back. The man stumbled onto the deck, teetering dangerously close to the stairs leading to the driveway.

Jonah thought that might knock some sense into him.

Instead, the man popped to his feet, appearing as spry as ever.

As soon as the man saw the beach umbrella lying there, Jonah knew exactly what he was thinking.

He was going to try again.

Before the man could grab it, Jonah snatched the umbrella from the deck. He held it up like a fighting stick used by martial artists.

As the man launched toward him, he collided with the umbrella. Momentum again threw the guy backward.

This time he hit the wood deck and rolled down two steps before catching himself on the railing.

Again, the attacker sprang back to his feet. Did this guy not feel pain? What was going on?

The man stared at Jonah, grunting as something nearly feral seemed to take over.

"And here we go again," Jonah muttered beneath his breath.

This time as the man lunged at him, Jonah used the umbrella to clothesline him.

The man fell flat on his back.

Jonah threw the umbrella down, grabbed the man, and flipped him onto his belly. Then he pinned the man's arms behind his back.

Jonah didn't have anything to tie up the man with, but he could hold him like this until backup arrived.

"I called 911," Rachel blurted, as if reading his mind. She stood in the doorway behind him, her arms crossed over her chest.

As she said the words, sirens sounded in the distance.

"Who are you?" Jonah kept his knee on the man's back, determined to find answers.

The man wriggled, surprisingly strong based on his size.

Was this guy on something? What was up with this superhuman strength? He had to be high.

"None of your business," the man muttered, his words slurred.

"Why did you come here?" Jonah continued.

The man's teeth were gritted, and foam formed at the corners of his mouth. "I . . . know who . . . you are. Evil people."

Evil people? What did that mean?

Before Jonah could ask more questions, the police zoomed to a stop in the driveway.

Cassidy was here.

Again.

If this happened too many more times, the police chief might as well consider herself part-owner of this house.

# CHAPTER SIX

THE MAN HAD BEEN PLACED in the back of the squad car as Cassidy took Rachel's and Jonah's statements in the living room. Her dad had heard the commotion and rushed out to check on them. He sat in a chair in the corner listening now, that familiar worry in his eyes.

Rachel rubbed her neck, which felt unbelievably tender and sore. It wasn't because anything physical had injured her.

It was stress. Anxiety always seemed to knit itself together in her neck and shoulders.

What a nightmare.

Cassidy let out a sigh as she turned to them, appearing tired—and rightfully so. "It's been quite the day."

Rachel frowned and nodded before leaning back

on the couch. "It sounds like it. I saw that couple on the beach earlier. You've had your hands full."

"Two more people down by the lighthouse displayed similar behavior," Cassidy admitted, her gaze growing wearier by the moment. "Two women this time who were on a trip with some of their old sorority sisters."

Rachel shook her head as surprise washed over her. She nestled more deeply into the couch, wishing the furniture would swallow her.

No such luck.

"What in the world is going on?" Jonah asked as he sat beside her.

"I saw something like this once." Cassidy's expression tightened. "Some people were on this drug called flakka. It was a psychosis-inducing hallucinogenic drug that made people act crazy."

"I've heard of that," Jonah murmured. "I think it was called the zombie drug or something, right?"

Cassidy nodded as something close to apprehension filled her gaze. "It was pretty scary, but the island got through that. We'll get through this as well. I just need to wait on those tox screens to give us some answers. If it's not drugs . . . then I'm not sure what it could be."

"Maybe it could be something in the water," Rachel suggested. "Do all of these people have hot tubs or pools at their houses? Some of the chemicals could have been tainted."

"Excellent idea. I'll look into it."

Rachel shifted, unsure if she should say this next part or not. She contemplated her choices and then decided it couldn't hurt to speak what was on her mind.

"Remember a couple of months ago, we had that incident where those men were trashing their rentals?" They'd been hypnotized as a ploy to distract police.

"I definitely remember. I thought that was an isolated incident." Cassidy tilted her head as she studied Rachel. "Wait . . . you don't think what's going on is connected with Ocean Essence, do you?"

Rachel pressed her lips together as she contemplated what to say. "I haven't seen anything suspicious going on there if that's what you're asking. But something about this whole situation makes me feel uneasy. Maybe it's the events from earlier today messing with my mind. I don't know. I just thought it couldn't hurt to mention it."

"No, you were right to remind me of that. I'll check on that too. In the meantime, if you think of anything, please let me know."

Cassidy left again.

A visit from the police to her house twice in one night? It was a little too much for Rachel's comfort, especially considering she'd seen Cassidy earlier in the day as well.

This wasn't normal.

As her dad disappeared to make some tea, Rachel turned to Jonah.

She'd been ready to send him away. But she knew the incident at her door had changed everything.

She suppressed a sigh as she looked up at him. "How about if I get the spare bedroom ready for you?"

He nodded, the relief in his gaze visible. "I'd feel a lot better if I stayed."

Rachel hated to admit it, but so would she.

———

Rachel didn't sleep very well. She had too much on her mind.

Before the sun rose the next morning, she hopped out of bed and saw her father off on his work trip.

Rachel had assured him that she'd let Jonah help keep her safe, and her father had finally agreed to go. But he was taking security with him, just in case.

Maddox King, a Blackout agent, had picked her dad up to take him to the airport. Blackout was a group of former military special ops guys who now worked private security. They were based out of

Lantern Beach and led by Cassidy's husband, Ty, and his friend Colton Locke.

In the meantime, Rachel got ready for the day.

But one question lingered on her mind.

What would today hold? It had to be better than yesterday, right?

She couldn't confidently say yes.

For starters, Jonah was here.

Then there was the gunman.

And the people acting crazy on the beach, and their possible connection with Ocean Essence.

Along with the man who'd attacked her father.

Plus, there were the disturbing phone calls she'd received.

A slight throb began at her temples. Yesterday's events offered a lot to comprehend.

The good news was she didn't have to go into work today.

Instead, she'd go to church.

She put on some white linen pants and a blue shirt before going downstairs.

To her surprise, Jonah waited near the front door in a button-up shirt and khakis.

She froze. She hadn't expected to see him. She especially hadn't expected to see him dressed and ready for church.

He seemed to read her mind and shrugged. "I

hope you don't mind. I planned on going to church anyway."

Rachel could only imagine the questions people would ask her. But she wouldn't tell him no. The church building wasn't her personal property. Everyone could attend services, and she shouldn't want to stop anyone from being there.

She glanced at her watch, desperate to turn away from Jonah before he read too much in her gaze. "I'm running late, so I guess we should get going."

Rachel tried to keep her thoughts focused and her emotions in check as they stepped out the door.

Jonah handed her a coffee in a travel mug. "Fixed the way you like it, with a splash of cream and two sugars."

"Thank you," she murmured, grateful for his thoughtfulness. A moment of longing filled her. She missed those days when she'd thought the two of them had a future together.

As soon as Rachel stepped outside, surrounded by an already hot summer day, she glanced around, instantly on guard. She saw only the neighboring houses. The vehicles in her driveway. Her sandy lawn. Thankfully, she didn't see anything that put her further on edge.

She prayed her day stayed this way—safe and normal.

"Do you mind if I drive?" Jonah asked as they lingered on the deck.

"Not at all."

He flipped his keys in his hands. "Good. I was hoping you'd say that."

He led her to the lime-green Jeep in her driveway.

"New wheels?" Rachel had seen the vehicle last night, but asking about it hadn't been a priority.

"Rental. They said it was all they had."

"I know you hated that." Rachel hid a smile. A vehicle like that fit Jonah to the T. It seemed to scream adventurous yet attractive and fun.

He opened the passenger door for her, and she climbed inside. As Rachel did, she caught a whiff of his spicy aftershave. She tried to brush away any of the tingling feelings his close presence brought.

She couldn't let herself go there.

But that would be easier said than done.

# CHAPTER
# SEVEN

JONAH HADN'T REALIZED JUST how much he missed the community church here in Lantern Beach. Not only did he like Pastor Jack Wilson, but he also enjoyed the fellowship.

Jonah hadn't thought he'd like living on Lantern Beach at first, but the island had grown on him. He'd never really settled in one place for more than a year at a time, due to his upbringing and then his military career. He thought he was meant to be a nomad.

Then he'd met Rachel, and all of those things had changed.

He had visions of the American dream complete with a house with a white picket fence and 2.5 kids.

But he'd been silly to let himself go there. To let himself imagine the possibilities. To pretend his life would ever be normal.

Despite how much he enjoyed being back at the church, Jonah remained on guard for the entire service, looking for anybody who might be out of place.

No one caught his eye.

That was a relief, at least.

He spotted so many people he recognized— friends he'd made while he was here. Hunter Bancroft and his girlfriend, Abby Mendez. Mac MacArthur and his wife, Tali. Colton Locke, who headed up Blackout.

Police Chief Chambers was also there with her family. Jonah considered asking her for an update after the service. But church didn't seem like the right time to ask about things like that.

As soon as the sermon ended and the last song had been sung, a flood of people came to talk to him and Rachel. Most of them didn't seem to know the two of them had broken up, only that Jonah had moved away. He wondered if that was because Rachel hadn't told them or if they assumed the two of them were back together.

He supposed it didn't matter. He'd left Lantern Beach, leaving Rachel to explain and pick up the pieces.

Maybe that wasn't fair.

Noelle Purdy paused beside him as they stood in the church's foyer. A man waited beside her. "It's so good to see you back, Jonah. This is my boyfriend, Gunner Mathias."

Jonah quickly observed the man with dark hair and a beard before shaking his hand.

Former military, if Jonah had to guess. There was just something about the way the guy carried himself that screamed he'd been through formal training.

A lot had happened since Jonah had left here, apparently. He was glad Noelle seemed happy. Jonah had gotten to know her some when she and Rachel had become friends.

"Did you get my text yesterday?" Noelle asked Rachel.

Rachel pressed her eyes closed. "Yes, I did. I'm sorry I forgot to respond. Things have been crazy."

"Don't worry about it. Just checking. Listen, could we all go to lunch together?" Noelle looked back and forth between him and Rachel. "I would *love* that."

Rachel looked as if she was about to object when Jonah spoke up. "We'd love to join you."

He didn't make it a habit of answering for someone else, but having lunch together would be a great way to keep his eye on Rachel. He wasn't sure how much she'd willingly let him tag along and keep watch over her. He'd need to look for those ripe opportunities, and this was one of them.

"How about we go to The Docks restaurant?" Noelle suggested. "I know you love The Crazy

Chefette and so do I, but it's a beautiful day, and I'd love to sit out by the water."

"That sounds perfect," Jonah answered.

Rachel cast him a dirty look that he ignored.

His phone buzzed in his pocket, and Jonah hoped it might be a message from one of his colleagues. He'd asked for information on that mystery person who'd reached out to Rachel twice via phone. His colleagues were trying to trace the number.

They needed to figure out if there was a connection between the call and what was happening here on Lantern Beach.

Noelle smiled up at them, either clueless or willfully ignorant of the tension between Jonah and Rachel. "Perfect. How about we meet there in twenty? Sound good?"

Rachel offered what looked like a forced smile. "That sounds great."

———

Rachel tried not to fume. But how could she not?

Why would Jonah answer for her? This was *her* life he was disrupting. Rumors would start. She'd have more explaining to do—and that was the last thing she wanted.

As soon as they were in his Jeep, she turned toward him. Her blood felt hot as it pulsed through her veins. "I'm not sure us having lunch together is a great idea."

He shrugged as if it weren't a big deal. "Not even after that man showed up at your door wielding an umbrella and foaming at the mouth?"

"That was most likely an isolated incident." After having time to think about it, she'd changed her mind after her earlier statement last night.

She now knew without a doubt that having Jonah by her side was too big a risk on her heart.

"It's just better if I learn to do things myself," she finished. "Enabling me isn't helping me."

"Protecting you isn't the same thing as enabling you. Besides, two are better than one. It's even in the Bible—two are better than one because they have a good reward for their toil. For if they fall, one will lift up the other . . ."

Great. He was quoting the Bible. How could Rachel argue with that?

"Rumors are going to start. People are going to think we're still together." She crossed her arms, settling in for a good debate.

"From the sounds of it, people at church already think we're still together." His unspoken question lingered in the air. *Why didn't they know?*

Rachel let out a sigh and ran a hand through her hair. "How was I supposed to explain that you chose your job over me without them feeling sorry for me or asking too many questions?"

"Rachel . . . it wasn't like that." Jonah's voice almost sounded pleading.

"On the contrary, that's exactly what it was." She practically dared him to deny it again. "Unless you just used it as an excuse to end our relationship."

"That's not it at all . . ."

Rachel let out a sigh, already tired of his excuses. She needed to change the subject. "Anyway, so instead, I just told them you had to go away for work. I figured I'd fill in the rest of the details later. Besides, it's not really anyone's business."

"It's not." His voice sounded serious and subdued.

Rachel hadn't expected him to agree so easily. She started to say more, to explain herself, but she stopped.

He understood.

At the moment, she simply needed to make the best of things.

Quietly, he started the Jeep and eased from the parking lot.

"So Noelle has a boyfriend now?" Jonah started as they headed down the road.

"Yes. Gunner's a really nice guy. Veteran. Lost his leg."

"Really? I couldn't tell. Noelle looks happy, so I'm happy for her."

Why did Jonah have to sound so sincere? It would be a lot easier not to like him if he was mean and miserable.

But he wasn't.

He never had been.

As she'd gotten to know him, she'd seen the hurts from his past. She'd sensed he'd never had a real support system in place.

She'd wanted to reach through that, to show him that stability was an option. That her arms were a safe place to fall.

But none of that mattered anymore.

Several minutes later, they pulled into a parking area near the boardwalk. Rachel dreaded having to put on an act during lunch. Dreaded pretending everything was okay in front of her friends.

But she'd get through this.

She always did.

Rachel only prayed today would be more peaceful than yesterday.

# CHAPTER
# EIGHT

JONAH MADE sure they got an outside table with shade that was situated against the building so he could watch everything going on around them.

Considering all that happened yesterday, he couldn't afford to let down his guard.

The Docks was a lovely restaurant located on the boardwalk. Their seafood was top-notch, and so were the views of the beach. Add to that the scent of the ocean as it swirled around them, and the aroma of Old Bay and garlic, and the place was a winner.

After they'd settled at the table and ordered, they chitchatted over glasses of water and baskets of cheddar-and-garlic biscuits.

The meal together seemed easy and casual like they'd done this a million times before.

But Jonah's thoughts continually wandered.

Gage had messaged him earlier, but Jonah hadn't read the text yet. When he had a moment, Jonah excused himself to view the message.

His colleague had traced that phone number Rachel had given him, and it pinged at a location in Arizona.

Jonah had also tried to call the number last night after Rachel went to bed, but no one answered. In fact, the number was no longer in service.

That seemed suspicious within itself.

During a break in the conversation, he cleared his throat. "I know this sounds like an off-the-wall question. But does Ocean Essence have any facilities in Arizona?"

Noelle and Rachel glanced at each other, both confused at the abrupt shift in conversation.

Rachel finally answered, "Not to my knowledge. Why?"

He shrugged. "I know it's an international company, so I was just curious."

But the look Rachel gave him made it clear she knew there was more to this.

As their food came, more casual conversation followed.

Ordinarily, Jonah would enjoy this. But not with everything that had happened within the past twenty-four hours.

As he took a bite of his crabcake, he glanced

across the boardwalk. A man wearing a baseball cap and sunglasses watched them from a distance.

A baseball cap and sunglasses?

Yes, a lot of people wore those.

But not everyone wearing them stared at Rachel.

That had to be the guy who'd grabbed her at gunpoint yesterday.

Wasting no time, Jonah threw his napkin on the table.

Then he darted toward the man.

———

Rachel could hardly breathe as she watched Jonah take off.

He'd seen something suspicious, hadn't he? His instincts were good. Danger must be close.

"Rachel?" Noelle stared at her from across the table as Jonah disappeared into the crowd in the distance.

Rachel tried to no avail to take a deep breath and remain calm. "I have a lot I need to explain some time."

"It sounds like it." Noelle frowned and glanced around as if worried.

Rachel knew Jonah was capable. But that didn't mean she wouldn't worry too.

That man who'd grabbed her yesterday had a

gun. What if he pulled it on Jonah? Put him out of commission? Or worse?

Rachel could hardly stand the thought of it.

Even though they'd broken up, she still had strong feelings for him. It didn't mean she had to act on them. But they were there like a wart she couldn't get rid of.

Gunner's gaze trailed to where Jonah disappeared. "Do you think he needs help?"

Gunner was not only former military, but he was currently in training to become one of Lantern Beach's new police officers.

"I . . . I don't know," Rachel stammered. "At this point, I'm not really sure of anything."

Gunner started to get up, then glanced at Noelle and settled back in his seat, as if he didn't want to leave her side in case there was danger nearby.

Thoughts and memories bombarded Rachel. The gun. The creepy phone calls. The people acting so disturbingly.

As Rachel remembered everything that had happened over the past twenty-four hours, she lifted up a prayer for Jonah.

# CHAPTER
# NINE

JONAH'S MUSCLES strained as he sprinted down the boardwalk.

He couldn't back down.

He needed to catch this guy. To figure out who he was and what he wanted. To figure out if he was associated with Amar or someone else.

As soon as Jonah stood from the table, the guy had taken off and now had a sizable head start.

It didn't help that the boardwalk was especially packed today.

As he reached the amusement park, he paused.

Where had the man gone?

Jonah stood there, ignoring the aroma of popcorn and cotton candy that floated around him. Such happy scents in such a tense situation.

The irony wasn't lost on him.

He had to find this guy before the man ruined these people's vacations.

Jonah peered over people's heads, trying to spot the guy.

But it was no use.

The man had either gotten away or he was blending in so well that he was unrecognizable.

His stomach knotted.

For all Jonah knew, the guy could have taken off his hat and sunglasses. Then Jonah definitely wouldn't recognize him. That was what Jonah would have done.

He continued searching the crowd. He didn't want this guy to get away.

But as he reached the end of the boardwalk, he finally paused.

Jonah hated to admit it, but this guy had eluded him. He'd somehow slipped away.

Jonah needed to get back to Rachel, just in case that man decided to head back toward her in some kind of bait and switch.

Gunner was there, but Jonah didn't trust anyone else to look after her.

———

Rachel released her breath when she saw Jonah heading back their way.

He was okay.

However, sweat covered his brow, and his jaw appeared tight.

She recognized that look.

He wasn't happy.

But he seemed to try to force his shoulders to relax as he sat down across from them.

Act like nothing had just happened? Good try. But the charade wasn't going to work with her.

All three of them stared at him, waiting for an explanation.

Instead of giving one, he picked up his napkin and placed it in his lap.

"Well?" Rachel finally asked.

He took a sip of his iced tea, appearing entirely too laid-back. "I thought I saw someone. It was a misunderstanding."

They all continued to stare at him, not quite believing his words.

Finally, he let out a breath as his resolve seemed to crumble. "I thought I may have seen the man who pulled a gun on you yesterday."

Noelle gasped and turned toward Rachel. "Someone pulled a gun on you?"

Rachel waved her hand, her cheeks reddening. "It was nothing."

She hadn't planned on telling her friends. There was no need to make a big deal about these things and make people worry about her. Besides, Noelle seemed so happy lately. Rachel didn't want anything to ruin her friend's bliss now that she and Gunner had found each other.

Jonah's gaze caught hers. "Sorry. I thought everyone knew."

"What happened?" Gunner narrowed his eyes with concern as he turned to Rachel.

With a sigh, Rachel explained the situation to them.

Their worry only seemed to deepen with each new detail. Wrinkles formed at the corners of their eyes. They glanced around. Their guard went up.

"You have no idea who it could have been or why?" Gunner leaned closer, his gaze intense.

Rachel shook her head. "I have no idea."

But when Rachel glanced at Jonah, she saw a new emotion cross through his gaze.

Wait . . . did Jonah know something she didn't?

That was how it appeared.

Rachel couldn't wait to catch him alone.

Because she had a lot of questions for him. Was there something he wasn't telling her?

If so, she needed to know the truth.

AS SOON AS they left the restaurant and climbed back into the Jeep, Rachel turned toward Jonah.

He had been expecting her to demand an explanation. He just hadn't wanted to share everything in front of Noelle and Gunner. He was used to keeping details private.

"What happened back there?" Her voice came out rushed yet hard.

He filled her in on the chase. "Unfortunately, I lost him."

"But you think it was the gunman who grabbed me yesterday?"

His shoulders shot up in a quick shrug. "That's my best guess. You didn't happen to see him, did you?"

She squeezed the skin between her eyes,

appearing both burdened and frightened. "I guess I wasn't looking. I thought I was being careful, but . . ."

Jonah had been highly trained to pay attention to these types of things. It was another reason he was glad to be here right now, even if Rachel didn't want him to be near her.

As air from the AC filled the vehicle, Rachel continued. "And why did you ask about Arizona?"

His jaw tightened. "My friend traced the number of the person who called you. The call was from Arizona. Near the Sonoran Desert. As far as you know, Ocean Essence doesn't have any facilities there, right?"

She shook her head. "Not that I know of. I mean, I haven't exactly studied everything about the company. It's so large with offices and facilities worldwide. But I haven't heard of anything relating to Arizona." Rachel paused and studied his face for a moment. "I just feel like there's something you're not telling me."

Jonah stared in the distance at the boardwalk and the individuals walking there. People continuing on with their normal lives.

Average, everyday US citizens. Many of them had probably saved their money for most of the year just so they could come to the island for a week to enjoy some time with their family.

Sometimes Jonah didn't feel like he'd ever be that person. It seemed too much evil existed in the world. Instead, he worked hard to make sure people like these vacationers could keep living the American dream, that these freedoms weren't destroyed.

He supposed everyone got a different assignment in the grand scheme of things.

This was his.

Most people couldn't face the reality that life was fragile. That their way of living was fragile. All it would take was one thing to go wrong . . . and everything they found comfort in could disappear.

He'd learned that lesson the hard way.

———

As they remained in the parking lot, Rachel refused to change the subject or let it drop.

Instead, she waited for Jonah to talk.

She wasn't going to let him off the hook this easily.

She followed his gaze and saw people who had no clue of the crimes occurring on the island. What Rachel wouldn't do to feel that kind of cluelessness.

Finally, she turned back to Jonah and repeated, "Is there something you're not telling me?"

She expected Jonah to look irritated or to run his

hand over his face as he tried to figure out what to say.

But he did none of those things.

Instead, he turned to her. "The truth is, in my line of work there are people I've made very, very angry. As a way of retaliating against me, I fear they're going to find you."

"What?" The word came out sounding breathless.

His expression remained solemn. "A job I'm working right now . . . it involves the leader of a terrorist group. We believe he somehow found a way to get onto US soil, and that he's planning something."

"That's terrible."

Jonah nodded grimly. "Yes, it is. Rumor has it that he knows who I am."

"How is that possible?"

"That's what I'd like to know also."

Rachel narrowed her eyes. "So, just for clarity . . . you think someone you encountered from your military career—an enemy—is now seeking revenge against you?"

He nodded stiffly. "That's right."

Rachel shook her head.

She hadn't expected to hear that. But she supposed his theory made sense. The scenario very well could be a possibility.

Against her will and despite the heat surrounding

her, she shivered. She supposed she didn't want to think about how deep this could possibly go.

Yet she couldn't afford not to, not if her life might be on the line.

Silence stretched a moment until Rachel finally cleared her throat. "I'd like to talk to Cassidy."

"To report we saw the man outside the restaurant?"

Rachel shook her head. "No—well, maybe that too. But I want to see if there are any updates on those people who were acting so bizarre at the beach. I'm not sure how much she can tell me, if anything. But I'm curious about whether they're connected to everything else that's been happening. It can't hurt to ask."

That wasn't true. Asking could lead to a lot of pain.

But Rachel was going to do it anyway.

# CHAPTER
# ELEVEN

POLICE CHIEF CASSIDY CHAMBERS slipped inside her house and into the office she'd set up there.

She normally tried not to work on Sundays and to reserve the day for church and family. However, she had a pressing matter that she couldn't stop thinking about. She wouldn't stay away for long from her family and friends who'd gathered outside.

But she needed to see something that couldn't wait.

She sat at her desk and opened a file on her computer. A moment later, pictures filled her screen.

Her officers had taken these photos inside the homes of each of the people who acted as if they'd lost their minds.

She nibbled the inside of her lip as she studied the images.

What did these photos all have in common? They'd already confirmed that these people didn't all have pools or hot tubs, so that ruled out Rachel's theory.

The people who'd acted as if they'd gone crazy yesterday had to have been exposed to something. She'd thought about flakka. Could that be it?

She wouldn't know until the tox screen results came back.

In the meantime, the people she'd brought in yesterday had been taken to a hospital in Raleigh until doctors could figure out how to treat them. Whatever was wrong, it hadn't worn off yet. Even worse, none of them were able to be questioned.

She sighed as she continued to scroll through the pictures.

What if something had been slipped into their food or drink? Or . . . maybe it could be bath salts or something of that nature?

Cassidy wasn't sure.

She just needed to find the one thing they all had in common.

She paused a moment and rubbed her eyes. Balancing being the police chief with being a wife, mother, and friend wasn't always easy. She couldn't do it without a lot of support and understanding from everyone in her life.

From outside her window, the happy sounds of everyone hanging out on the beach drifted inside to her. Ty had grilled some tile fish and shrimp. Everyone had brought sides to share. Once they finished eating, they'd play some volleyball.

It was her favorite day of the week by far, and she was so grateful to have everyone in her life.

She'd come to Lantern Beach out of desperation. But what she'd found here were good people who'd become family.

More than anything, she wanted to protect this community she'd come to love so much.

That was why she had to figure out what was going on.

She just couldn't let these incidents go. She needed to find answers ASAP.

Especially when she thought about something like this happening again in the future. People might get hurt next time.

Many more of these incidents, and tourists would be fleeing these shores. Without tourism, industry on the island would die.

Or the implications could be far more wide-reaching and serious.

Cassidy would look at the photos one more time, and then she'd pass this task off to a fresh set of eyes.

She squinted and enlarged one of the photos.

It was a picture of a bathroom in one of the houses.

On the counter, there was a bottle of lotion called Natural Defiance, an anti-aging cream.

Cassidy thought she'd seen that bottle before.

Quickly, she scrolled through the other photos again.

She paused at pictures of a bedroom dresser with cosmetics placed on top.

Sure enough, the same brand of lotion was there.

She clicked on a search engine tab and plugged the name of the lotion.

Her lungs froze when the results came up.

The lotion was manufactured by Ocean Essence.

That couldn't be a coincidence.

Quickly, she began looking through the rest of the photos.

She needed to be sure this lotion was the link she'd been looking for.

But she felt confident it was.

# CHAPTER
# TWELVE

RACHEL KNEW Sundays were the police chief's day off, but she called her friend anyway.

Cassidy had said she'd been just about to call Rachel, and she asked if Rachel could stop by her place to chat.

Jonah and Rachel pulled up to Cassidy and Ty's beach cottage, a familiar place where both Rachel and Jonah had attended Bible study before he moved. The home had six colorful cabanas out back used for Ty's nonprofit.

Cars lined the driveway, so Jonah had to park closer to the street.

They climbed from his Jeep and were greeted by Kujo, a golden retriever.

After properly rubbing the dog's head, they took the stairs toward the front door, and paused.

A group of people played volleyball on the beach, some feasted on fish near a grill, and others just sat on the sand enjoying the ocean breeze.

In fact, Noelle and Gunner had joined the group since they'd been at the restaurant.

Cassidy spotted Jonah and Rachel standing on the stairs and came over, her baby girl, Faith, on her hip.

Or maybe Faith wasn't such a baby anymore. If Jonah remembered correctly, the girl was about a year and a half now.

"Thanks for coming by." Cassidy nodded toward her screened-in porch. "Why don't we step inside and grab some water? It's getting warm out here, but at least there's a nice breeze."

They moved into the screened-in porch. As they did, Jonah spotted Ty as he stepped from the house, a platter full of more fish to be cooked in his hand.

"If it isn't Jonah Gray." Ty extended his hand. "I thought I saw you at church this morning, but I didn't have a chance to make it over to you. Good to see you, man."

"Good to be here," Jonah said. "I just wish the circumstances were different."

Ty sobered. "Agreed."

Despite the circumstances, Jonah did miss this. The normalcy of it all. The community. The down-to-earth good people.

But Jonah reminded himself again that he could

never have a normal life. He'd say it was the way he'd been raised—in foster care.

But that wasn't it.

No, instead it was the way he'd been *created*.

Reality seemed morbid, but it was true. Jonah had been selected by the government. Gone through rigorous testing and training. Those things had made him into the highly trained operative he was today.

People watched movies that romanticized the concept of someone being transformed into a hero like Jason Bourne. But there was nothing romantic about the things Jonah had been through, things that had made him into the person he'd become.

Once Ty disappeared over the dune with the platter, Cassidy turned to them. "You have questions about the incident that happened yesterday on the beach?"

Rachel nodded. "I hate to interrupt you on your day off. But I've been concerned."

"You have every right to be. It was unnerving to see what happened. Two more incidents occurred later on as well—so six all together have been reported." Cassidy shifted Faith from one hip to the other.

"What?" Rachel gasped, shaking her head. "What is going on?"

"Actually, I wanted to talk to you about that anyway." The light in Cassidy's eyes dimmed.

Jonah's spine straightened at Cassidy's words.

He anticipated what was coming, and he didn't like the scenarios running through his head.

"We're still waiting for the tox screen to come back," Cassidy explained. "But in the meantime, we were able to examine the rental houses where these people were staying. They were all tourists. We found one object within the houses that was similar."

"What was that?" Jonah held his breath as he waited for her answer.

"A bottle of anti-aging lotion called Natural Defiance . . . manufactured by Ocean Essence." Cassidy glanced at Rachel. "Is there anything you can tell me about this product?"

Rachel opened her mouth but then shut it again as questions swirled in her gaze.

———

"What in the world could Natural Defiance have to do with what's going on?" Rachel murmured.

Honestly, she had no idea. What sense did that even make?

Natural Defiance was the number one selling skin lotion in the world and practically a household name. It was the product the company was founded on.

"It has to be a coincidence," Rachel added.

Cassidy tilted her head. "You're a scientist. Do you really think this is happening by chance? When you look at all the evidence, the anti-aging lotion is the only constant variable. It's the only thing that makes sense right now."

"Our products go through rigorous testing for safety," Rachel said. "The only thing I can think of is that maybe a box of this product was tampered with after it was delivered to a store. Maybe someone put some type of drug that could be absorbed through the skin in the products here on Lantern Beach."

Rachel stared off in the distance and frowned at the thought.

Cassidy shifted Faith again. "Now that you mention it, we need to collect any of this lotion on the island, just to be safe. If any more cases of this pop up and we confirm it's the lotion, I'll need to see if a recall alert can be issued. Is there a way you can figure out which locations carry it and how much was delivered?"

"Our production facility isn't here on the island, but I can see what I can find."

"In the meantime, I'll send my officers to collect whatever is left on store shelves." Cassidy rubbed Faith's back as if she didn't like the idea that an over-the-counter product could be harming innocent people.

Neither did Rachel.

She wanted to help people, not harm them. If the

company she worked for had anything to do with this . . . then her fears would be confirmed.

Ocean Essence was up to something.

"Did you call Dr. Hensley?" Rachel turned toward the ocean, relishing the cool breeze coming from it.

Dr. Hensley was her boss at Ocean Essence. He and his wife, Margaret, had moved to the island several months ago. Margaret, however, with her high-class taste, was having trouble adjusting to small-town living.

In fact, rumor had it that she'd gone back to the DC area for a while.

No one at the lab knew if she planned on coming back or not. But Dr. Hensley hadn't looked particularly happy lately. Some theorized Margaret was having another plastic surgery. From the tautness of the woman's face, she'd already had plenty.

"No." Cassidy frowned. "That's what I wanted to talk to you about."

Rachel held her breath as she wondered where Cassidy was going with this.

"I'm not ready to mention this to anyone else who works at Ocean Essence yet." Cassidy stepped closer and lowered her voice. "I just figured out the lotion might be the connection. Right before you came, I made a few calls to neighboring PDs to see if they were having any similar issues. So far, no one else has reported any problems."

That was good news, at least, Rachel mused.

"If other people are in danger, then I need to let the proper authorities know." Cassidy kissed the top of her daughter's head. "But I don't want to cry wolf too early either. I need more proof. Either way, I'm afraid if I mention this to anybody at Ocean Essence that any evidence will be destroyed as soon as they catch wind that we're onto them."

"You might be right," Rachel said.

Jonah nudged himself closer. "What are you asking Rachel to do exactly?"

Cassidy pressed her lips together before frowning. "I'm hoping she might secretly look into things at Ocean Essence."

Before Rachel could respond, Jonah did. "You could be putting her in greater danger."

Cassidy's expression remained serious, as if she understood the gravity of the situation. "It's like I said, if I confront the leadership or employees at Ocean Essence, there's a good chance they'll lie and destroy evidence. I need someone on the inside to help me."

Rachel expected Jonah to argue again, but he didn't. Probably because he knew Cassidy's words were true. Rachel was their best bet of finding any answers.

She remained quiet a moment as she thought over the possibility. Cassidy's plan made sense. But it was risky, and snooping could mean putting her life and career on the line.

Cassidy lowered her voice. "I don't want to do anything to put you in danger. But I can't think of another way. You're smart, and I trust you. I can't say that about a lot of people who work at the company. So just think about it, okay? But we don't have a lot of time. I'll need your answer soon."

Rachel nodded, already knowing she was up for the challenge—especially if it meant protecting others. "I will. Thanks for trusting me with this information."

CASSIDY INVITED them to join the crowd at the beach, but Rachel and Jonah declined.

Jonah had too much on his mind.

Cassidy and Faith had joined the rest of the group, but Jonah and Rachel remained on the screened-in porch talking.

He turned to Rachel. "I think you helping Cassidy is a bad idea."

"But that's the only idea that holds merit." Rachel locked gazes with him and didn't blink or look away.

Neither did he. "There has to be another way. Someone else can look into it."

"Who else? You and I both know if anyone gets wind of this . . ."

"There are always alternatives." He let out a long breath and shifted his thoughts, not wanting to argue right now. "Do you know anything about this lotion?"

She shook her head. "I was in on the initial launch of the reformulated product, but then it was handed off to someone else so I could focus on the dermatological side of the company."

"What about the ingredients? Anything weird?"

"No, everything is pretty standard—nothing strange about them. No whale vomit or human blood or anything."

"Human blood?" He raised his eyebrows.

Rachel shook her head. "Believe it or not, that is used in some beauty treatments. In fact, Dr. Hensley was one of the pioneers in those so-called vampire facials. Anyway, that's not really important right now."

"Maybe not." Jonah shifted. "Who's overseeing the project?"

"A man named William Morey, I think. He's a little strange but nice. He's smart. Single. From Philly originally. Nothing about him has ever raised any red flags."

"Is he working here in Lantern Beach?"

"As a matter of fact, he is." Rachel nodded.

Jonah's mind raced. Maybe they should give this guy a visit.

Then again, they couldn't tip their hand.

Their hand? Jonah chided himself.

This wasn't his case or Rachel's case. It was Cassidy's.

Jonah had been called here to protect Rachel, not to investigate.

But it was hard to stay out of it, especially since Rachel's life might be on the line.

Before they could talk about it more, his phone rang.

It was Gage.

Jonah couldn't put off his call . . . especially if Gage had more information about that phone call from Arizona.

———

Rachel stared out over the ocean as she tried to wait patiently to hear what Jonah's phone call was about.

But with everything going on, patience was hard to come by.

The only comfort she felt in the situation came from the gentle ocean breeze that washed over them. Something about the salty air always made her feel calm, including right now.

She just hoped that sense of calm would remain with her for a while.

Several minutes later, Jonah ended the call and turned to her.

"That was my contact," he explained. "He's been

researching the area where that phone call pinged from. There's almost nothing out there but miles and miles of emptiness and desert."

"I'm surprised there's even cell phone reception if it's that desolate."

"You and me both. Anyway, my friend—Gage—has a contact in the area, a guy named Jesse, who works at this place called Vanishing Ranch. Gage got Jesse to go check out the location. I thought for sure there wouldn't be anything, that this was a wild goose chase. Instead, he found a facility out in the middle of the desert. He said the building looked new, like something that had been constructed probably in the last six months."

Rachel's heart beat faster as she tried to form a picture in her mind of what might be going on. "Did they find out what kind of facility it was?"

"It turns out the place is owned by a company called Velocity. They only filed their paperwork to incorporate three months ago."

Three months ago? She stored that fact away as she created a mental timeline. "What kind of company are they?"

"They claim to be in the medical technology business."

"Was this Jesse guy able to look inside?"

"No, but he saw three cars parked out front.

However, he didn't see anyone coming or going while he was there."

"Is he going to keep looking into it?" Rachel rushed.

"He's going to see if he can find anything out and call me. It's better if someone else can look into this other than me, because it would take all day to fly out there and rent a car to get there myself."

"Makes sense." Rachel let out a breath. "Who could be responsible for this?"

"I have enemies. Terrorists. Gangsters. Evil men."

She shivered at the thought. "Like who?"

"How much time do you have?"

She stared at him. "There are that many?"

Jonah nodded. "Unfortunately, yes."

"That's not comforting." She let out another sigh before nodding toward the stairs. "I guess we should go."

"Back to your house?"

"No, to the lab." Her gaze locked with his. "We don't have any time to lose. But first, I want to get a bottle of this lotion myself so I can test it."

JONAH GRIPPED Rachel's arm as they headed down the staircase.

This conversation wasn't finished yet.

She glanced back at him, her hair twirling around her in the breeze and challenge in her gaze.

He returned the look. "I'm not sure going to the lab is a good idea."

Her gaze remained cool and unyielding. "You can come with me."

"You know the company keeps track of everyone who comes and goes. You told me that much after the incident back in March. If anyone asks, how are you going to explain why I'm there?"

"No one there knows we broke up, only that you were out of town on a job." She shrugged. "I don't like drama or for everyone to know my business."

It didn't feel quite as simple to Jonah. "But they're still going to think it's weird if I go to work with you, aren't they?"

"Not if I explain I left some work in my office that couldn't wait."

Jonah stared at her another moment, not liking this idea.

But it was the only idea, wasn't it? They needed answers and what better time to find them than while the lab was officially closed?

Finally, he nodded—though he still had reservations. "Let's go then."

A flutter of surprise rippled through her gaze, but she nodded.

They went back to his Jeep and headed down the road. First, they stopped at the general store. There were still three bottles of the lotion on the shelf.

Jonah bought all of them.

Then they headed toward the lab, which was about twenty minutes away on the southern end of the island.

They pulled into an empty lot, the sight of which made Jonah feel a little better.

At least no one else was here.

For now.

Memories hit him upon seeing the building.

Memories of when he and Rachel had been dating.

He'd been such a fool to let her go. And he knew that.

He'd broken up with her in order to avoid putting her in danger.

But maybe that risk was unavoidable, just like Rachel had said. Living was risky.

Either way, Rachel opened her door, her brazenness surprising him.

Nothing was going to stop her right now, was it? She was on a mission to right a wrong and protect the innocent.

That fact made him admire her.

And fear for her.

His throat tightened.

Before she got too far ahead of him, he hurried after her.

As they walked toward the door, Jonah prayed this was the right choice.

———

Rachel nodded at Axel, the Blackout agent on duty. Agents took shifts guarding this place as an extra layer of security.

Axel called hello before continuing to pace the outside perimeter.

She then used her biometric handprint to get into the building. Jonah followed right behind. As soon as she stepped into the reception area, she paused and glanced around the quiet space.

It appeared no one else was here.

So why did she still feel so nervous?

Rachel hurried across the open office area where most of the assistants worked and stopped by her office doorway. She unlocked the room, led Jonah inside, and then shut the door behind them.

She wasn't sure why she felt so uneasy, but she did. No one else was here. Yet she was fully aware that cameras monitored this place all the time.

She just needed a moment to compose herself in the privacy of her office before they enacted the next part of her plan.

"What's next?" Jonah gazed at her as they remained by the door.

Her throat went dry at the sight of him. They were standing close. Too close.

Close enough that she could smell his spicy after-shave. That she could see the flecks of gold in his blue eyes.

If things had been different, Rachel might reach up on her tiptoes and plant a kiss on his lips.

But she couldn't do that anymore. She'd never again know what it was like to feel his lips against hers. To experience the explosions taking place in her chest and her heart.

Rachel had never felt with anyone else the way she felt with Jonah.

Safe. Loved. Protected.

A big part of her mourned that loss.

Another part of her mourned that it hadn't been real.

She cleared her throat, shifting her thoughts into safer territory.

Maybe.

"I need to get into the room with all the classified information. That's where the files on this lotion should be stored."

"Whenever someone goes into that room, is an alert sent out to management?"

She nibbled on her bottom lip. She remembered that safety feature that had been put in place after another incident had happened here in the lab. Hensley had been especially vigilant since then.

"Yes, so I'll have to come up with an excuse as to why I went in there," Rachel told Jonah. "But I'm working on a project now that requires access to that room so I should be fine."

His jaw hardened as he listened. "What do you want me to do?"

"I need you to let me know if anyone else comes in. I should be able to fumble my way through an excuse. But ideally, I'd like to keep this quiet."

"I can stand guard."

She stared up at Jonah another moment before nodding and gripping the door handle again.

"Let's go." She opened it, glanced around again to confirm no one was there, and then they headed across the office area.

At the door, she punched in her code and then used a biometric retinal scanner to get into the secure room.

The lock clicked, and she opened the door.

Bracing herself, she gave one last glance back at Jonah.

"I'll be here if you need me," he murmured.

No doubt he was remembering what happened last time the two of them were in this lab together.

Rachel had almost died at the hands of a greedy killer.

Considering that fact and what was going on now, she was glad Jonah had her back.

But the sooner she got this done, the sooner they could get out of here.

With that thought, she shut the door, leaving Jonah to stand guard outside.

She hoped she could find the information she needed—not just for her sake, but for everyone else who also might be a target.

# CHAPTER
# FIFTEEN

JONAH LEANED against the wall as he looked across the lab.

He wanted to believe this was just an innocent skin care and cosmetics company.

But from the moment Ocean Essence had arrived on this island, he'd believed there was more to their presence than that.

The secrets this place held . . . they practically saturated the air.

Jonah didn't like the idea of Rachel being in harm's way. But he knew having her dive deeper was one of the best means of finding the information they needed.

He glanced at his watch. Probably only five minutes had passed—if that.

But it felt like an hour.

Was Rachel having a hard time finding what she needed?

She was capable. If that file was in there, she'd find it.

Still, another part of him wanted to be in there right beside her.

Maybe he was being overprotective. Did women really want to be safeguarded? Or did they just want to thrive on their own?

Maybe it was a combination of both. He wasn't sure.

But another part of him knew personal preferences and niceties didn't matter. Rachel's safety was his first priority even if his protection offended her.

He stiffened when a shadow passed by the front doorway.

Was someone else here?

His lungs froze as he stared at the windows waiting for more signs of movement.

As the front door began to open, he paced away from the authorized personnel only room. Standing outside the door would look too suspicious.

Instead, he walked toward the vending machines in a nearby nook. He'd pretend like he was purchasing some water.

Just as he held up his credit card to the machine and pushed the button, a man stepped inside the lab.

Someone Jonah had never seen before.

The guy appeared to be in his thirties and was probably about forty pounds overweight. He wore glasses, and his head was mostly bald.

The vending machine released the water bottle, and it clunked to the bottom.

As he did, the guy jerked his gaze toward Jonah. His eyes widened, and he froze.

"Didn't mean to scare you." Jonah held up his water. "Just getting a drink."

"Who are you?" the man demanded, his entire body braced as if he might fight. "What are you doing here?"

"I don't believe we've met. I came in with Rachel Atwood." Jonah extended his hand. "I'm Jonah Gray."

His shoulders relaxed just slightly. "So that's why I saw a Jeep out front. I thought maybe someone had broken down and left it here over the weekend." The man hesitantly returned his handshake. "William Morey."

Jonah's heart beat a little faster when he realized who this man was. This was the guy who'd worked on that suspect lotion. "Nice to meet you."

William glanced around. "Where's Rachel?"

"She ran to the bathroom. I'm waiting for her so we can hit the road again. I think she wanted to grab some files she left here so she can work on them tonight. You know how she is. A total workaholic at times."

William seemed to loosen up a little. "I can see her working at all hours."

"I guess you might be that way too since you're here on a Sunday."

He shrugged noncommittally. "I've been called a workaholic before. But mostly I just wanted to get ahead for the week also. You know how that goes."

"I do. I won't keep you any longer." Jonah took a step back. "Have a good day."

As William began walking toward the other side of the building, Jonah slowly strolled toward Rachel's office.

How would she get out of the room without being seen?

Jonah wasn't sure, but he needed to warn her.

As soon as he was in her office, he texted her.

William's here.

A moment later, Rachel texted back.

Still trying to find exactly what I need.

Still? Why was it taking so long? Then again, Rachel probably had a lot of files to go through. Apparently, many of Ocean Essence's formulas weren't even kept on the computer for fear of a hacker obtaining them.

Jonah glanced outside again, shutting the door to the office slightly. Then he waited.

A moment later, more footsteps sounded nearby. He peered out the door, careful not to let William see him.

The man emerged from his office and glanced around nervously before walking toward the top-secret room.

He couldn't be going in there now, could he?

But the next moment . . . William paused beside the door and leaned toward the retinal scanner.

And Jonah realized that Rachel could very well be caught red-handed.

———

Rachel's phone buzzed again.

What now?

She glanced at the screen.

Jonah's message made her eyes widen.

William heading your way.

Panic surged inside her, and she quickly put her phone on silent.

She glanced around the space.

William was the last person she wanted to catch her in here right now, especially with the files that she had in hand.

She ducked under a desk and pulled the chair tight. She drew her knees to her chest, praying she wouldn't be seen.

A few seconds later, the door opened.

She watched someone step inside.

William. She recognized him by the jeans and loafers he always wore.

Why was he coming in here?

She watched as he paced toward the filing cabinet —the same one she'd just been going through.

He flipped through some files. Grunted. Flipped through more.

Then he paced back and forth before slamming the drawer shut.

Was he looking for the files Rachel had? The files on Natural Defiance?

Her heart pounded in her ears.

She knew Jonah probably had to be beside himself right now.

But so far William hadn't spotted her.

As long as the man didn't come this way, she should be okay.

Almost as if William could read her thoughts, he turned.

He started toward the desk.

Her heart raced.

Would he find her?

Rachel could barely breathe as he stepped closer and closer.

# CHAPTER
# SIXTEEN

JONAH FELT beside himself as the minutes ticked past.

More than anything he wanted to burst from the office and get Rachel out of there. For all he knew, William could be a killer, and he could be hurting her right now.

Jonah was powerless to stop anything since he couldn't get into the room. Even with all of his strength and training—and even with his Sig—it would do him no good in this situation. Not with the security system Ocean Essence had in place that prevented people from accessing that room.

He pinched the skin between his eyes with two fingers as he stood in Rachel's office. Coming here had been a bad idea. He should have tried to talk Rachel out of it. But she was just so stubborn . . .

*Lord, what should I do?*

Just then, the door to the classified documents room opened.

He straightened, hardly able to breathe.

Remaining in the shadows, he watched as William stepped out.

Glanced around.

Closed the door.

As the man took a step down the hallway, Jonah's gaze narrowed.

Was that blood on his hands?

The air left Jonah's lungs.

What had that man done to Rachel?

---

As William stepped from the room, Rachel released a breath.

That had been close.

Quickly, she texted Jonah to let him know she was okay. She didn't want him to do anything rash.

William had picked up a beaker and dropped it. When he cleaned the shards up, he must have cut his hand. He'd said some choice words and then Rachel had seen a few drops of blood hit the floor.

She thought for sure as he cleaned up his mess that he'd see her.

But he hadn't.

Still, she'd been keenly aware that he could have very easily hurt her, and no one would have been able to stop him in this room.

Flashbacks of an incident that had occurred here back in March whirred through her mind, causing her muscles to tighten.

She'd nearly died in here when she'd been trapped with a madman bent on revenge.

Now she had to figure out a way to get out of here without being seen. If William spotted her leaving, it would look especially suspicious now since he'd just been in here. He would know Rachel had been hiding.

She sent a text to Jonah.

Let me know when the coast is clear.

Then Rachel stood from her hiding place. She tucked her files under her shirt, just in case.

Finally, several minutes later, another message appeared on her screen.

Everything is clear but be quick.

Staying light on her feet, Rachel slowly opened the door and glanced at the space around her.

She saw no one.

She gently shut the door, made sure it was secure, and then rushed to her office.

As soon as she stepped inside, hands clamped around her arms.

She gasped as worst-case scenarios filled her mind.

Then she realized it was just Jonah.

Her heart raced out of control as she stared up at him.

At once, she realized that she wanted to be in his arms. To enjoy his kisses. To find comfort in his presence and friendship.

She willed herself not to think that way. It wasn't healthy. It would only set her back.

Yet . . . there he was.

In front of her.

Looking as handsome as ever.

"Are you okay?" Jonah stared into her eyes.

Rachel quickly nodded and tried to get her thoughts under control. "I am. But that was close."

"Too close." His voice hardened as he said the words. "Did you get what you were looking for?"

She pulled the files from beneath her shirt. "Right here."

His shoulders seemed to slump with relief before he nodded toward the door. "Let's get out of here. I've had enough of this place to last a lifetime."

Rachel wasn't going to argue with his statement.

Because lately, her dream job was feeling more like a nightmare.

JONAH QUIETLY LED Rachel from the lab and back to his Jeep.

His heart still pumped hard with adrenaline as he headed down the road.

That had been close.

He was about to ask her what she'd found in the classified room when he glanced in the rearview mirror.

Headlights appeared behind him.

Normally, Jonah might not think anything of the sight. But this road was secluded with no houses. So where had that vehicle come from?

"Jonah . . . ?" Rachel glanced behind her. "Something's wrong, isn't it?"

"I'm not sure." His grip on the steering wheel tightened. "There's a car behind us."

"Do you think someone has been watching us?" Her voice cracked with fear.

"It's always a possibility."

She leaned back and pressed her head into the seat behind her. Her breathing sounded labored as her anxiety seemed to build.

He wanted to reassure her that everything would be okay, but he couldn't.

The vehicle sped, now close enough that Jonah could no longer see the headlights.

"Hold on." His throat tightened as he pressed the accelerator harder.

It was just as he feared.

Someone was following them.

More than following them.

If he had to guess, someone was trying to send a message.

As soon as the thought fluttered through his mind, he felt a bump.

The car had hit them.

Rachel gasped beside him. "Jonah . . ."

"I've got this." He'd been through every defensive driving course available. The tricky part would be trying to keep not only Rachel safe but also any other innocent bystanders they came across. Thankfully, it was late so most people were in for the night.

But still . . .

He accelerated more as the vehicle came at them again.

He couldn't let this guy have the upper hand.

He needed to act—now.

Before Jonah could second-guess himself, he braked and jerked the steering wheel hard to the left.

The tires squealed.

The rear swung around as the Jeep did a 180.

They now faced the oncoming vehicle.

"Jonah . . ." Rachel gripped his arm as fear rippled through her voice.

"Just give it a second . . ."

As he watched, the other driver slammed on his brakes.

Jonah climbed from the Jeep, grabbed his gun, and took cover by the door.

Then he stared down the other driver, daring him to make another move.

He hoped this risk paid off.

———

Rachel watched as Jonah stared at the vehicle.

What was he doing?

What if the man tried to run Jonah over?

This all seemed like a bad idea.

Tension crawled up her spine and shoulders, embedding itself there.

Jonah was trying to stop this before it went any further.

Rachel prayed that wasn't a mistake.

She could hardly breathe as she waited.

After what seemed like an eternity, the other driver suddenly accelerated.

She gripped the armrest beside her as she anticipated the worst.

Would he hit Jonah?

Her gaze remained riveted to the scene.

The car came closer . . . closer . . .

Then it swerved and sped past at the last moment.

She released her breath as the driver backed down from the confrontation.

Jonah was okay. His risk had paid off.

It could have turned out so much differently.

She craned her neck. Maybe she could see the license plate. Maybe they could at least report this guy.

But there wasn't one.

Jonah stared after the other driver another moment before climbing back into the Jeep. His shoulders and jaw were tense, making it clear that he wasn't happy.

"I don't know whether to pat you on the back or scold you." Rachel leaned toward him, her voice growing stern. "What if that guy had run you over?"

"I figured he was just trying to send us a message. Besides, if I didn't end this here and now, then it was going to lead to a chase through town in which other people would have been put in danger. I couldn't let that happen."

She drew in a shaky breath, thankful for his quick thinking and experience.

But with every passing moment, it became more and more clear that someone was watching her and waiting for the right opportunity to enact some kind of plan.

Jonah turned the Jeep around, and they started back to her house. Several minutes later, they pulled into her driveway. He quickly checked the back of the Jeep for damage.

Rachel spotted a small dent in the bumper. "You'll need to report that when you return the vehicle."

"I will. It's a good thing I got extra insurance. Besides, that situation could have been so much worse."

Jonah put his hand on the small of Rachel's back as he led her toward the house.

She couldn't deny the shock of electricity that rushed through her at his touch. It had always been that way with Jonah.

The attraction was unmistakable.

He ushered her inside and locked the door behind

them. Then he checked out the rest of the house before giving her the okay that it was safe.

Rachel released a breath she didn't even realize she'd been holding until just then.

Jonah paused in front of her in the living room. "I know you're anxious to review those files. How about if I make us tea?"

Tea . . . the thought of it brought back so many memories of the time the two of them had spent together. Drinking tea. Playing Scrabble. Sharing about their lives. Dreaming about their future together.

Rachel shoved those bittersweet memories aside. This wasn't the time to get nostalgic. Too much was on the line to get her emotions involved right now.

Instead, she nodded. "That would be great."

Then she took the files and sat on the couch, ready to begin reviewing what information she might find.

TWO HOURS LATER, Rachel was still looking through the files.

Jonah rested on the couch, trying to be laid-back. He knew answers weren't always easy to find, and he needed to be patient.

But given everything that had happened, he was on edge.

Rachel had already gone through two cups of turmeric and cinnamon tea. Jonah had downed his own peppermint tea, a drink that gave him a moment of regret.

A moment of regret? Who was he kidding?

Ever since he'd called things off with Rachel, all he'd felt was regret. He'd simply kept reminding himself that this was what was best for her. He had to keep her safe.

Yet sometimes that task seemed impossible.

Finally, Rachel sighed. She pulled off her reading glasses and used her palms to massage her eyes.

She looked exhausted. As she should be. It was already past midnight, and they'd had a long day.

"Well?" he asked.

She turned toward him and frowned. "I hate to say this, but I don't see anything suspicious in these notes. According to what I'm reading, every ingredient in that lotion is approved by both the FDA and our company."

Jonah tried to hide his disappointment. Not that he wanted there to be a dangerous ingredient in the lotion. But he wanted answers. He wanted this to make sense so they could put this threat behind them.

"What about the delivery of products to Lantern Beach? Were you able to see any of those files?"

"I accessed them on my computer," she said. "But again, there was nothing suspicious. The man who delivered the products to the island is the same one who always does. Maybe someone paid him off or something. I have his name to give to Cassidy."

"It's a start."

Rachel let out a sigh and let her head drop back against the couch. "I feel like this is going nowhere."

He started to reach over and squeeze her hand but stopped himself. No need to stir that up again—

even though everything about touching her would feel natural, would feel right.

That didn't mean it was a good idea right now.

"We'll keep looking," he assured her. "There are answers somewhere, right? Every contact leaves a trace—Locard's Exchange Principle."

Rachel gave him a questioning look at his use of scientific terminology.

"I use forensics on the job." He shrugged. "What can I say? Maybe I have a scientist buried down deep inside me."

"Maybe," she said with a laugh.

A moment of silence stretched between them.

Suddenly, she propelled herself into an upright position. "I need to test this lotion. It's the only way I can get some answers. I was hoping the files would reveal something but . . ."

Jonah agreed that that seemed like the next step. But why did she seem so anxious about it?

"Where do you propose we do that?" he asked. "I'll see if I can help you get set up."

But as Rachel looked at him, he knew he wouldn't like whatever she was about to say.

"I need to go back and test the lotion at Ocean Essence," Rachel announced. "It's the only place that makes sense."

Jonah shook his head, making it clear where he stood on the issue. "Absolutely not. It's too risky."

"Not if I go now. William should be gone. No one should be there."

Jonah hesitated. "If you go back tonight then they're going to have another record of you entering the building."

"The company never frowns on workaholic habits. The more time they can squeeze out of us, the better. That's all Hensley will most likely think."

"Are you sure?"

She nodded. "This shouldn't raise any eyebrows."

"Why can't you just use another lab?"

Rachel stared at him and shrugged. "Where am I going to find another lab that has the equipment I need to use? Even if I find one, what am I going to say to convince them to let me use it? Even if I were to find a space I could rent, there would be a waiting list and paperwork to fill out. Ocean Essence is the only lab that makes sense. It's the only place I have full access to."

Jonah stared at her, questions and doubt still in his eyes.

She locked her gaze with his. "It's the only way. If

we don't get some answers, then danger is just going to keep following us."

He didn't argue with her statement.

Jonah stared at her, and she waited for his response.

She knew she couldn't do this without him. She needed someone to watch her back.

She didn't trust anyone else with knowing what she was about to do . . .

Rachel pressed her lips together as she waited for Jonah to respond.

# CHAPTER
# NINETEEN

JONAH HAD a lot of reservations about Rachel's idea.

But he also knew going back to the lab was the only way to get answers in a timely fashion.

First, they really needed to think their plan through. The problem was it was already after midnight, and they'd lose the privacy that nighttime allowed them if they waited too long.

He rubbed his neck, feeling the tight muscles there. "We need to really talk through these details."

Hope filled her gaze as she nodded. "I'm ready."

For the next fifteen minutes, they talked logistics.

Then they left the house again. But Jonah continued to keep watch, looking for anyone who might be lingering.

He saw no one.

He drove back toward the lab, parked, and headed inside.

Rachel stared up at him with her big, brown eyes as they stood at the stairway leading to the upstairs laboratory. "You stand guard down here. At the first sign that someone is coming, text me."

Jonah would do that.

Thankfully, the Blackout agent guarding the place only patrolled the perimeter and didn't come inside. Jonah could have probably trusted him enough to let him know what was going on. But he didn't want to get anyone else involved.

Not yet.

Besides, he knew if anyone else showed up here, then it would already be too late.

He prayed that didn't happen.

He'd come here to keep Rachel safe, not lead her into more danger.

———

Using an elemental analysis machine, Rachel hoped to determine both the elemental and isotopic composition of Natural Defiance. Even more so, she needed to see if these results matched what was in the files.

The machine would break the ingredients down into atoms and then send the analysis to her computer.

The problem was, the process wasn't always fast, and time wasn't on their side right now.

Still, she prepped the lotion, then put the samples into the machine, and waited for the analyzer to do its job.

As she passed time, she studied the files on the anti-aging lotion again.

But nothing in the paperwork was suspicious.

She frowned as she leaned back in an office chair in the laboratory.

Something was wrong, and she had to figure out what.

They were running out of time.

Finally, the machine beeped and quieted.

Then the computer dinged, signaling she had her results.

With trembling hands, she clicked on the report.

Leaning closer to the screen, she studied the answers.

But . . . something wasn't right.

This analysis didn't match the paperwork she'd just been studying.

How could that be?

She needed to find out what each of those extra substances in the composition might be.

One thing was certain: someone had tampered with this lotion.

But what had they done to it? And why?

# CHAPTER
# TWENTY

JONAH REMAINED near the front door. There were only three ways to access the building. The main door at the front and two emergency exit doors on the sides.

But if anyone opened the emergency exit doors an alarm would sound.

No one should know they were here.

With any luck, this whole visit would go unnoticed.

He and Rachel had decided that 4:00 a.m. was the latest they'd leave. Some people liked to come into the office early, around five, and the two of them couldn't chance being here if that happened.

He wished he could be upstairs with Rachel. See what she was doing. What she'd discovered.

But he needed to be down here keeping a lookout.

He hoped and prayed all this wasn't for nothing.

But there were no certainties right now.

Whatever was happening, it felt big. Bigger than him and bigger than Rachel.

Just then, he thought he saw a shadow move on the other side of the glass of the front doors.

He straightened.

Was someone outside?

He considered his options.

Stay in here and wait for someone to possibly come inside.

Or go out there and check it out himself.

He didn't like either option. He hoped he'd simply been seeing things.

Then he thought he saw the shadow move again.

He couldn't take any chances.

Quickly, he texted Rachel.

We might have trouble.

He watched the screen until he saw confirmation that the message had been read.

Rachel replied:

Wrapping up now. I found something.

A sense of victory surged through him. Maybe this wasn't a wasted effort after all.

But the bad feeling in his gut continued to grow.

Jonah wouldn't put it past whoever was responsible to follow them here tonight for some evil purpose.

Carefully, he opened the door from the office area into the reception area. Remaining along the edge of the wall, he crept to the front door.

Then he stepped outside, gun drawn.

But as soon as he did, he realized he was surrounded.

———

Rachel heard the commotion outside, and her heart rate kicked into high gear.

What was going on?

She quickly cleaned up everything and shoved the samples and printouts into her bag. She needed to leave the lab the way she'd found it.

But it might not matter.

Because trouble may have found them.

She prayed Jonah was okay.

Then she rushed down the steps.

As soon as she reached the first floor, she saw flashing lights.

Flashing *red and blue* lights.

Nausea rose inside her. Were the police here?

She stepped toward the door, dreading what she might find.

Where was Jonah?

Was he outside?

Her limbs trembled as she stepped that way.

She couldn't cower inside while he faced whatever was happening alone.

Her head spun when she pushed the door open and saw three police officers surrounding Jonah, guns raised as he slowly lowered his weapon and set it on the ground.

As the breath left her lungs, Rachel raised her hands in the air. "It's okay. He's with me."

But the officers didn't back down.

Instead, Officer Dillinger walked toward Jonah. He secured Jonah's wrists with handcuffs and began to read him his rights.

What?

Rachel could hardly breathe.

She had to make this right!

"I work here," Rachel argued. "Why are you arresting him? He's with me."

Cassidy stepped from the shadows and took Rachel's arm. "I'm sorry, Rachel. But you have the right to remain silent . . ."

Her head spun as everything went still around her. "What are the charges?"

"Corporate espionage."

# TWENTY-ONE

RACHEL LOOKED up and saw her boss, Dr. Hensley, step into the interrogation room. The man was in his late fifties and on the shorter side, with a wiry build. He had an olive complexion and thick salt-and-pepper hair.

His personality was brisk, and everything he said and did was measured and guarded.

The first time Rachel had met the man, she hadn't liked him. But she'd come to appreciate his stand-offish demeanor.

She'd probably be the same way if she were in his shoes.

Maybe he could explain this mix-up because Cassidy, who stood in the corner with her arms crossed, hadn't said anything.

"Rachel . . ." He paused in front of her.

She nodded curtly. "Dr. Hensley."

"I never thought I'd see you here."

"I never thought I'd be here." She kept her voice even, though part of her wanted to snap. "You care to explain why I've been arrested for corporate espionage?"

He pulled the metal chair out from beneath the table and lowered himself across from her. "I've suspected that something might be going on at the lab and someone might be trying to steal secrets. I had extra security stationed out of sight near the facility. I suspected that whatever was happening occurred during the nighttime hours, and that someone had managed to bypass our security system on more than one occasion."

"You think that was me?" Rachel pointed to herself, surprise lacing her voice. "I was there tonight trying to help, not trying to start more trouble."

His expression remained stoic. "I wish I could believe that. But there's a lot on the line right now. I checked the footage from earlier tonight. It was wiped. That's when I decided to put some extra eyes on the place, and I saw you show up."

"It was wiped?" Rachel asked. "You think I did that?"

"Were you at the lab earlier as well?" He stared at her as he waited for her answer.

Her cheeks flushed. "I was. But so was William."

"William also? I suppose we should question him then as well." But based on his tone, Hensley didn't think William could be guilty of anything.

Just Rachel.

"Dr. Hensley, you've got to believe me." Her voice rose with desperation. "I'm trying to help."

"Why don't you tell him what you were doing at the lab tonight then?" Cassidy stepped closer, an unreadable expression on her face.

But that clearly seemed to be the police chief's way of giving Rachel permission to share information from their earlier conversation.

Rachel let out a sigh as she contemplated exactly what she wanted to say. She knew there was no need to keep the truth to herself.

"With all that's been happening on the island, I suspected that someone might have messed with the ingredients in one of our lotions," Rachel admitted. "When I looked at the files, I didn't see anything strange. So I decided to examine a sample of Natural Defiance myself."

"And?" Dr. Hensley stared at her as he waited for the answer.

"My suspicions were confirmed. I know we use algae as one of our anti-aging ingredients. However, the algae sample I found in this lotion appeared to be toxic."

"What?" His voice rose with surprise.

"And there's more." Rachel remembered the odd results she'd found. "I'm nearly certain someone put jimsonweed in this formula as well."

"Why in the world would someone do that?" Dr. Hensley shoved his eyebrows together, not bothering to hide his doubt.

"Probably because jimsonweed can stimulate production of white blood cells and neutralize various free radicals. As you probably know, this plant has been used for medicinal purposes for years by Native Americans. However, it can also give people hallucinations, among other things."

"So you're saying there are two additional ingredients in this lotion than what are supposed to be?" Hensley appeared more and more apprehensive with every word he spoke. "One of them is toxic, and another makes people see things that aren't there? How would that even happen? We have strict measures in place to prevent such things. We take every precaution to ensure the safety and quality of our products."

"That's what I'm trying to figure out. At least I was before I was arrested." She tilted her head and gave him a pointed look.

Dr. Hensley didn't say anything. Instead, he let out a deep sigh before running a hand over his head. "I can't believe a nightmare like this could be happening. Why would someone even want to do this?"

"I've been looking into this matter as well," Cassidy said. "We've had some tourists with peculiar and dangerous behavior here on the island. I linked all of them back to Nature's Defiance. I asked Rachel if she would look into it."

"Why didn't you come to me?" Dr. Hensley demanded.

"Before I made any accusations, I needed more proof. The state crime lab was working a little too slowly for my liking. That's when I asked Rachel about this."

He grunted. "I should have known about this beforehand."

"You may be right," Rachel said. "I was going to approach you next, but then this happened."

"While we're on the subject, I should have been alerted that you had extra security set up in the area," Cassidy said.

Dr. Hensley's eyes narrowed, and he didn't look happy about being called out.

Cassidy continued. "Why the extra security?"

"After everything that happened back in March, I thought it was important—at least until things settle down."

"Your employees do have access to the lab whatever the time, day or night, correct?" Cassidy stared at him as she waited for his answer.

"In theory." His face reddened.

Cassidy nodded slowly but confidently. "Then Rachel wasn't doing anything wrong by being there. If you want to press charges, you'll have to pursue other avenues. Rachel is free to go."

He let out a huff.

Rachel hoped Dr. Hensley would believe her. She couldn't afford to lose her job over this. She had to get this figured out. Too much was at stake.

Cassidy turned to Rachel. "But I would like both of you to stick around so I can ask more questions."

Rachel glanced at Dr. Hensley as she waited for his response.

She desperately prayed this bad situation didn't turn any worse.

And where was Jonah? Was he being given this same consideration?

What if her plan to go to the lab somehow ended with him being in legal trouble?

Her mind raced.

If that was the case, Rachel would do whatever it took to fight for him . . . especially since tonight had been her idea.

Jonah was relieved an hour later when he found out any charges against him and Rachel had been dropped and he was being released.

Since they'd both been driven to the station in separate squad cars, Officer Dillinger drove them back to Jonah's Jeep.

He and Rachel hadn't had a chance to talk yet, but the glances they exchanged said enough.

This situation was perilous, to say the least.

"Sorry about that back there," Dillinger said as he drove.

"You were just doing your job," Jonah said. "Can't fault you for that."

"That lab has been nothing but trouble since it opened here," Dillinger said. "No offense to you, Rachel."

"No offense taken." She crossed her arms as she stared out the window in the back seat, a forlorn expression on her face.

Rachel was clearly upset about all of this. Jonah couldn't blame her.

What he really wanted was the opportunity to talk to her in private. Even though he trusted Dillinger, no one else could be privy to the conversation he needed to have with her. But that talk would have to wait.

A few minutes later, they pulled up to the Jeep and thanked Dillinger.

After Dillinger left, Jonah and Rachel sat in the Jeep. But Jonah made no effort to leave.

He'd been so worried about her. All he wanted was to hold her close.

But he couldn't do that.

Instead, he knew he shouldn't, but he grabbed Rachel's hand.

He wanted to connect with her on some level.

Rachel didn't pull away.

That was a good sign, at least.

"Are you okay?" Jonah gazed at her, worried about her emotional well-being right now.

"I think so." She nodded slowly. "At least we know someone tampered with that lotion. It's a start, right?"

"Yes, it is."

"What should we do now?" She stared up at Jonah as if she hoped he had the answers.

"I think we should get back and rest. Maybe some sleep will do us good."

"I agree."

"But Rachel . . . I really think you should back off and let Cassidy take over."

Her gaze met his. "How can I when the lives of innocent people are on the line? I can't look the other way. You wouldn't either."

Jonah didn't say anything. He couldn't argue because she was absolutely right.

# CHAPTER
# TWENTY-TWO

RACHEL DEPOSITED her purse by the entry and watched as Jonah locked the door behind them.

Maybe tomorrow things would make more sense, one way or another.

She remembered how she felt when Jonah had grabbed her hand.

Like everything was right in the world again.

Like she'd found her soulmate.

Except Jonah *wasn't* her soulmate. He'd broken up with her. He'd chosen his job over her.

Sometimes Rachel felt as if they needed to have a conversation about that. But she wasn't sure how to bring the subject up, especially with everything else going on. Besides, these other issues were so much more serious.

So she kept quiet.

It was better if she put that part of her life behind her.

For now, Rachel liked the idea of getting some sleep.

But she also knew she was too wired to rest right away. Her mind bounced all over the place after everything that happened.

As she tried to calm her mind, she thought some things through.

She had no doubt some of her coworkers would hear about what happened tonight. That she was arrested. Accused. Humiliated, really.

How could she just go in to work today as if everything were normal?

There was obviously more to it than that.

She stepped into her living room and flipped the light switch on the wall.

As the room brightened, she gasped.

A man sat in a chair near the fireplace.

He stared at her as if he'd been waiting impatiently for her to arrive.

Rachel stumbled back as fear filled her, and a scream escaped.

———

As soon as Jonah saw Rachel stumble backward, he knew something was wrong.

Then she'd screamed.

A strange man sat in her living room. The man had darker skin and was probably of Latino descent. His dark hair was thick, and his build short but stocky.

Jonah stepped in front of Rachel and grabbed his gun from his waist.

"Who are you, and what are you doing here?" Jonah aimed his Sig at the man.

The intruder tensed and rose to his feet, hands in the air. "I don't mean any harm."

"Then what are you doing inside this house?" Rachel demanded.

"I needed to talk to you without being seen, and this was the only way."

"Breaking into my house was the only way?" Rachel's voice lilted with accusation.

"Please, if you'll let me explain then I think you'll understand." The man's voice cracked.

"You have five minutes before I call the cops." Jonah kept his gun raised.

"I understand." Tension stretched across the man's gaze. "You have to know that the only reason I'm here is because I'm desperate."

"Clearly." Jonah had a biting edge to his voice.

The man's gaze went to Rachel. "Ms. Atwood, you're the only one who can help me. I came here all the way from Arizona just to find you."

THE MAN'S words raced through Jonah's mind.

Arizona.

Was this guy connected with that facility out there? It couldn't be a coincidence.

"Let's hear him out." Despite her words, Rachel didn't break her death stare she had on the man.

Jonah lowered his gun slightly. "Start talking."

"My name is Santino Lopez," the man said. "I work for a company in Arizona named Velocity. For the past three months, we've been conducting clinical trials for Ocean Essence."

"Ocean Essence doesn't have any facilities in Arizona." Rachel's voice trembled just slightly.

Sweat spread across Santino's forehead. "The work is contracted. Anyway, the people in charge told the test subjects being used for trials that they'd be given luxury accommodations and be paid handsomely for their time and trouble. But they had to commit six weeks of their lives to the project."

"That's not the way it normally works, but okay . . ." Rachel's voice trailed with skepticism.

"I thought it was strange because many of the people they were using for these trials were almost nomadic. They had no families at home waiting for them. One was an out of work actor, more of a hobbyist really because I think he was only in one commercial. One was homeless. One was a college student who wanted to spend the summer hiking. Then there was a mother and her older teen daughter who'd just been evicted. You get my drift, I guess."

"Go on." The man had Rachel's full attention. She stared at him, barely breathing.

Santino shifted and rolled his neck. "But I was concerned about how some of the trials were going. I noticed a distinct change in the people's behavior, and it just wasn't right."

"What kind of change?" Rachel asked.

"They were acting as if they were out of their minds, almost rabid."

Rachel stepped closer, a new eagerness to her voice. "Did you tell anyone about what you were witnessing?"

"I tried to tell my boss, but he brushed me off and said I was reading too much into this. That I should let them do their job and that I should do mine. My official job was an assistant supervisor." He rubbed his throat as his breathing became more shallow. "Then one of the people started going crazy. Like out of their mind crazy. They took this one guy, Henry, to the hospital . . . supposedly."

"Why do you say *supposedly*?" Jonah's words sounded terse.

Sweat spread across Santino's forehead. "I mean, I was walking behind the facility, and I came upon a grave. The winds had been particularly strong for several days, and the gusts . . . they must have uncovered the body." His voice cracked. "It was Henry. He'd been shot."

"What?" Rachel gasped.

"Was anyone else harmed?" Jonah asked. "Or did anyone else disappear?"

"A couple of people were forced to leave . . . at least, that's what my boss said. Said they weren't good candidates for the trial after all."

Rachel gasped beside him. "Wait . . . was one of them a woman?"

"Yes, why?"

The phone call, Jonah silently mused. Someone from this facility had somehow managed to get a cell phone, find Rachel's number, and call her.

But what had happened to that woman?

Was there only one dead body?

Jonah suspected there might be more that hadn't yet been discovered.

"Someone called me—a woman. She pleaded for my help. But the number was disconnected, so I had no way of knowing who she was or how I could help." Rachel drew her arms over her chest.

"One of the people who disappeared was Sharon. It could have been her. She's the one who came to the program with her daughter."

"How old was her daughter?" Rachel's voice sounded wispy with tension.

"Probably eighteen. Maybe nineteen. They wouldn't accept anyone younger."

"Did they experiment on the daughter?" Rachel's words came out faster.

"They did. And it didn't go well. Then the mother disappeared."

Rachel's hand covered her mouth.

"People were freaking out—especially the new people who came in—after they saw some of the earlier participants," Santino said. "But my boss wouldn't let anyone leave by their own free will. The test subjects all signed contracts saying they'd lose everything if they did."

"So why did you come here?" Jonah asked.

His gaze locked on Rachel's. "I decided to go straight to the source."

"The source?" Rachel narrowed her eyes.

Santino's gaze locked onto hers. "Since your name was on the trial, I came here to beg you to help. You've got to shut this down and figure out how to help these people!"

"What are you talking about?" Rachel's voice lilted. "My name was on it?"

"You're listed as the scientist in charge. Your name was on the contract. It's probably the reason that woman knew to call you. This was your project. This is all your fault! That also means you're the only one who can stop it."

Rachel shook her head. "No, it's not my project or my fault. I have nothing to do with this. I'd never even heard of Velocity until yesterday."

"I'm begging you to put an end to this!" Santino's voice cracked with desperation. "If not, I'm afraid this formula—and those men—will kill more people."

This guy's story just kept getting worse and worse.

"Who else did you try to get help from, besides the police?" Jonah asked.

"I went to my boss again, hoping he could explain. He acted concerned but told me to stay quiet while he tried to find out more information. I believed him. But the next day, they sent me on an errand to the store. On the drive there, someone tried to shoot me."

"What?" Rachel gasped.

"I managed to escape. But I know it was someone from the company trying to silence me." Santino's gaze locked with Rachel's. "You've got to help me. Please. If the wrong person gets their hands on this formula . . ."

Rachel's throat tightened.

That was her thought exactly.

But it might already be too late.

———

It would take Rachel a while to process everything Santino had told them.

Not to mention the fact her heart was still racing from finding a strange man in her house.

Santino stood, wiping his palms on his pants. "I'm sorry to break in like this. But I couldn't risk being caught. I don't know if anyone followed me or if they're tracking me somehow. I know I sound paranoid, but . . . you haven't seen what I've seen."

Part of Rachel wanted to insist that Santino remain here at her place. But she wasn't sure what that would prove, or that any of them would be any safer for it.

"I wish I could help you," she started. "But I don't have anything to do with this. I think I'm being set up."

Sweat covered his forehead. "So there's nothing you can do?"

"I didn't say that," Rachel said. "I'll do my best to stop this."

"Is there anything else you can remember that might help us?" Jonah asked.

Santino's eyes flittered back and forth. "The name Draco kept coming up back at Velocity. I'm not sure what it meant or if it's important. But the way the higher-ups whispered about him made it seem relevant."

"We'll see what we can find out." Rachel's gaze latched onto his. "Where are you staying?"

"It's better if no one knows. I parked down the street. I know this seems so cloak and dagger, but you've got to understand the stakes of the situation." He rubbed his palms on his pants again.

"I do," Rachel said. "You were brave to come here. But what if I need to get in touch with you again . . . ?"

He took a business card from his pocket and handed it to her. "You can call me here. I need to figure out what to do next."

Jonah walked him to the door. As soon as Santino was gone, Rachel sank into the couch and tried to process everything he'd told her.

Jonah joined her. "What do you think of that?"

"To be honest, I don't know what to make of it. It's almost too much."

"I'm trying to think everything through." Jonah stared at the wall in front of him almost as if lost in thought. "So somehow this formula was created, maybe with good intentions at first. But the effects are devastating. Why go through the trouble of setting up this fake clinical trial? That's what I don't understand."

"That's a good point. Why not just simply discontinue the formula, note it's a combination we can't use, and move on?"

Jonah met her gaze. "Because what if the wrong person realized how powerful this formula could be? Or if they wanted to use it for nefarious purposes?"

At the question, everything in the room seemed to go still.

Rachel couldn't stop thinking about whether or not Jonah's words might be true.

# TWENTY-FOUR

JONAH WAS FIXING breakfast that morning when he heard someone coming down the hallway. He looked up and saw Rachel standing there . . . but she wasn't still in her pajamas or even dressed casually.

Instead, she wore dark slacks with a white shirt.

He frowned as he scrambled some eggs. "Where are you going?"

She let out a quick sigh, her chest appearing tight. "To work."

His throat constricted. "That seems like a really bad idea."

"It's the *only* idea I have if I want answers. I tried to do a search on the computer for 'Draco,' but I didn't find anything."

Jonah shook his head again. "I really don't like the idea of you going back to the office. I called Gage, my colleague, and he's going to do more research for us. Why don't you just take a sick day from work?"

Her jaw hardened. "I can't do that. I'm not going to hide. We need answers before more people are hurt, and you can't argue with that."

Jonah stared at Rachel as he tried to come up with a plausible rebuke. But he knew he wouldn't be able to dissuade her. She was too stubborn, too determined.

She glanced at her watch. "By the way, I texted Noelle, and I'm going to meet her for breakfast. I wanted a few minutes alone to talk to her."

He turned the burner off, his eggs done. He'd made extra for Rachel, but he could easily finish them all on his own. "Where are you meeting?"

"On the boardwalk."

"I'm not sure that's a good idea either." All his instincts were on alert. He didn't want to be overly protective, but how could he not be? This was Rachel's life they were talking about.

Rachel looked at him a moment, her lips twisting with thought. "I assume you're going to want to come. That's fine. But I would like some privacy when I talk to Noelle. You could be nearby if it would make you feel better."

"It would make me feel a lot better. When are you meeting her?"

"In thirty."

He raised his plate. "Let me eat and get changed. Fifteen minutes, and I'll be good to go."

———

When Rachel arrived at the boardwalk, she spotted her friend sitting on a bench facing the ocean.

They'd chosen to meet here because it was out in public. A lot of people were always around. Yet they could have some privacy as they talked.

That was exactly what she wanted.

Jonah had driven her here, and now he lingered in a nearby gazebo where he could keep an eye on them. But if Rachel were honest with herself, she welcomed his protectiveness. It was good to know that someone else had her back.

But she also reminded herself not to get too used to feeling like this. Jonah had come and gone from her life before, and the likelihood he would do the same again was strong.

She couldn't afford to put her heart on the line by dreaming about what could be.

She sat on the bench beside her friend, feeling more on edge than she'd like.

"Hey there," Rachel started.

"Rachel!" A smile lit Noelle's face. She reached into a brown paper bag and handed her a bagel. "For you."

In return, Rachel handed her some coffee she'd grabbed at Beach Bound Books and Beans.

Noelle had become a good friend to Rachel since she'd moved here. Since she worked at the lab, she'd also become a confidante.

Noelle glanced to the side and nodded toward Jonah. "Bodyguard?"

Rachel hid a smile. "That's what it feels like sometimes."

"If you're going to have a bodyguard, then you want him to look like that." She offered a playful laugh.

Rachel stole a glance back at him. "Maybe. Unfortunately, it's more complicated than that."

Noelle's smile disappeared. "I know it is. If you don't mind me asking, what's going on? I thought you guys had broken up."

"Jonah didn't think he could do his job and date me, so he chose his job. But now he's back."

"And he's back because . . . he wants to win your heart?" Noelle tilted her head as if trying to read between the lines.

Rachel glanced around again and then leaned

closer. "Not exactly. There's more going on than that. After what happened on Saturday, my dad called him. Jonah was worried about me, so he came here to Lantern Beach to keep an eye on me."

"That doesn't sound like someone who wants to move on from a relationship." Noelle raised her eyebrows pointedly.

"It's complicated. I hate saying that, but it's true."

"It's clear he still has feelings for you and that you still have feelings for him."

Rachel shrugged, unsure how she felt about that statement. She definitely knew she still cared about him. But she wasn't sure how he felt. After all, he had left, choosing his job over her.

That had stung more than she wanted to admit.

"Feelings don't matter," she finally said. "Feelings will get me nowhere except to heartbreak—something I can't afford right now."

Noelle smiled, almost sadly. "I get it. If you ever need to talk . . ."

Rachel smiled, trying to show her gratitude for Noelle's friendship. "I might take you up on that sometime. But for now, there's something else I need to talk to you about."

"What's going on?" Noelle shifted toward her and took a sip of her coffee.

Rachel surveyed the area around her one more

time, just to make sure no one familiar was lingering close.

Still, she lowered her voice as she said, "It's about the lab. Something is going on, and I need your help."

# CHAPTER
# TWENTY-FIVE

JONAH KEPT an eye on Rachel as she and Noelle chatted.

He didn't like this arrangement. He wished that he could just lock Rachel away. If only it was that easy. But it wasn't.

Besides, the world needed her brilliance. Not only her smarts, but her smile and kindness. She had too much to offer to be kept isolated.

But the only other alternative was that she was in the open and exposed.

At least that was how it felt.

As he stood there, trying to enjoy the breeze from the ocean, his phone rang.

It was Larchmont.

He groaned. He wished he could ignore the call from his boss, but he couldn't.

Instead, he jammed the phone up against his ear, still keeping an eye on the area. "Morning. What's going on?"

"That was my exact question for you." As usual, Larchmont's voice came over the line sounding hard and unyielding. "How's the situation there in Lantern Beach? The one that you were willing to drop everything for?"

"It's more serious than I ever suspected."

Larchmont paused. "I'm sorry to hear that. Does that mean you're not going to be back anytime soon?"

Jonah glanced at Rachel again as she and Noelle laughed about something. "It means . . . I don't know. I don't feel right leaving now when there are so many things unresolved."

"We have unresolved assignments we're working on also. Do I need to remind you this is your job and your responsibility?"

Anger burned through Jonah at his boss's words. "I understand. For basically my entire life, I've never had any personal time. It's always been about work and the military and my job. But right now, I need to take care of this. It's nonnegotiable."

Larchmont paused another moment. "Is that right? Good to know. But I can't guarantee you that I'll have a job here waiting for you when you get back."

Jonah's breath caught. But Larchmont's threat wouldn't make him back down. "I'm sorry to hear that. I hope it doesn't come down to that. But for now, I'm needed here."

"Very well then." His voice sounded especially terse. "Have it your way."

Larchmont ended the call, and Jonah slipped the phone back in his pocket. He almost expected to feel disappointed. But he didn't.

His job *had* been his entire life for . . . well, for his entire adult life.

But was that really what he wanted? Was there a possibility he could use his skills and still have a personal life? That he could still have Rachel at his side?

That was the question that continued to haunt him.

Rachel was the best thing to ever happen to him. He'd never met another woman like her.

He hadn't wanted to move away and leave her.

But fear had taken hold. He figured she'd be safer with him gone.

At least that was what he thought at the time. The only thing he was sure of now was that he'd been a fool to walk away from her.

But wasn't he being given a second chance now? If that was the case, would Rachel ever really consider taking him back?

He wasn't sure.

But he wanted to explore the possibility.

He scanned everything around them again—the vacationers, the shops, the beach.

That was when a familiar face caught his eye.

He blinked.

And the man was gone.

Maybe Jonah had imagined it.

But he'd thought for sure that he'd just seen Amar Ravish.

If that was true . . . then they really were in trouble.

———

"I've never heard the name Draco before." Noelle narrowed her eyes as she listened to Rachel, her bagel all but forgotten.

"I hadn't either." Rachel frowned. Part of her wished her friend might have heard of the name. That maybe she'd have some answers.

But that didn't appear to be the case.

"Rachel . . ." Noelle narrowed her eyes as her voice softened. "None of this sounds good."

"It's not good. I'm not even sure I should be telling you any of this. The last thing I want is to put you in danger."

"I appreciate that, but you can trust me." Noelle's

gaze locked with Rachel's. "Nobody needs to know we've been discussing any of this. I'll keep this to myself."

Rachel's jaw hardened as she realized how risky it was to be sharing any of this with Noelle. "Please do. For your sake."

"So what are you going to do?" Noelle studied her friend's face.

Rachel pushed a lock of hair behind her ear as she contemplated what to say. "I'm going to see what I can find out."

Before they could say anything else, a shadow fell on them. Rachel's muscles instantly tensed as she anticipated the worst.

She looked up and saw Rex Houghton standing beside them.

Relief filled her—but clearly Jonah had the opposite reaction.

He visibly tensed as Rex moved closer.

The man was in his thirties with a ruddy complexion and thick, light-brown hair. He dressed and carried himself in a way that made it clear he had money and thought highly of himself.

Not long ago, he'd been a victim after an attempt to resurrect a deadly disease.

The memory of that near catastrophe replayed in Rachel's mind. Things had been so tense here on the island.

It seemed like a lot of trouble had come to Lantern Beach recently. Some of it was centered around the lab and the people working there. Why was that?

"Well, ladies . . . I didn't expect to see you here. But it's a lovely day to enjoy the outdoors." Rex grinned and stretched his arm to display the ocean, almost as if he'd created it himself.

"I agree." Noelle's voice suddenly sounded more professional and not as welcoming as it had earlier. "What brings you out here?"

"I just like to stretch my legs before work."

"There's no better place to do it than here on the boardwalk, is there?" Rachel really wanted to move this conversation along. She had a lot to do and a lot to talk about.

"No, none at all." His gaze flickered back and forth between them as if he were trying to think of something else to say in order to keep the conversation going.

Finally, he nodded. "Well, I'll let you two finish your breakfast. Have a great day."

As soon as he was out of earshot, Rachel turned to Noelle. "He still has a thing for you, even though you're dating Gunner now, doesn't he?"

"I don't know." She shrugged before frowning. "But it seems like he always goes out of his way to talk to me."

Almost as soon as Rex had moved to the island, he'd shown interest in Noelle. The two had gone on a few dates before Noelle met Gunner.

Rex was some type of business mogul, though Rachel wasn't sure exactly what kind of field he was in. She hadn't asked questions. But the man made it clear he was very successful.

The memory of his brush with death filled her thoughts again.

He'd had those seizures and that rash because of a disease. Was that what they were facing here on the island again? Or was this something different?

She didn't know.

Rachel glanced at her watch and let out a sigh. "It looks like we both need to get to work."

"Yes, we do." Noelle nodded toward Jonah. "Is he going with you?"

Rachel followed her gaze and studied Jonah a minute. He looked so handsome as he stood there with his hair blowing in the wind. He leaned casually —at least that was how it appeared—against the wooden post of the gazebo, but Rachel knew that at a moment's notice he could spring into action.

Her heart panged with a moment of grief, of loss.

What they'd shared together had been beautiful.

But now it was gone, and there was no need for her to dwell in the past.

Then she remembered that Noelle was waiting for an answer.

"I think I might just have to bring Jonah along with me to work—but only for practical purposes." If only she could get the man out of her heart as quickly as he'd walked out of her life.

AT 7:37 A.M., Cassidy Chambers got a call from dispatch.

A body had been found on the side of a busy road.

Possible hit-and-run.

She headed to the scene now with Officer Dillinger.

Trouble always seemed to show up on these shores, no matter how hard she fought to keep this island safe.

They pulled to the side of the road where Officer Leggott waited for them along with the passerby who'd discovered the body. This part of the island was filled with vacation homes—all of which were at capacity for the summer.

Onlookers gathered nearby, trying to get a glimpse of whatever had happened.

This wasn't exactly the thing summer memories should be made of.

Cassidy braced herself for whatever she might be about to see.

Plastering on her most professional expression, she walked toward the ditch.

Looking down, she spotted a man in his forties with dark hair and a receding hairline. She'd never seen the guy before.

"What do you know about what happened?" she asked Leggott.

"He was already dead when I arrived on the scene. Based on the bruising and the positioning of the body, I would guess it's a hit-and-run."

"Estimated time of death?"

"Based on the rigor, I'd guess that it happened sometime during the early morning hours."

Cassidy studied the area. "We'll need to check and see if anyone nearby has any cameras that captured anything. In the meantime, was there an ID on this guy?"

Leggott nodded. "I found a driver's license. The guy's name is Santino Lopez."

Cassidy hadn't heard the name before. "Where is he from?"

"Arizona."

Arizona? That was a long way for someone to come here on vacation. But they'd had people come from other countries, so it did happen.

She stared at the man another moment, hating that his trip here had ended this way.

Did this man's death have anything to do with the other occurrences on the island?

Could the person who hit him have done so because they'd also gone crazy—this time behind the wheel?

It was a possibility she needed to consider.

"We need to find out where he was staying and if he has family," Cassidy told Leggott. "Did he have a cell phone on him? Maybe we can find some numbers on that."

"I'll get on it." Dillinger stepped away.

Cassidy stared at the victim another moment, compassion welling in her.

"I'll find answers for you," she muttered. "If it's the last thing I do."

# TWENTY-SEVEN

JONAH SAT in a corner chair in Rachel's office and turned away from his research, needing to clear his thoughts a moment.

He scanned the office, a place he'd been before. Floor-to-ceiling windows lined one wall and a built-in bookcase the other. Right behind her desk, there used to be a picture of the two of them together.

The photo had been taken on the beach as the sun set, smearing peach and purple in the sky. The smile on her face had been luminous.

Now that picture was gone.

A knot lodged in his throat at the thought.

He shifted his gaze to Rachel.

He couldn't help but marvel at how beautiful she was. Not only beautiful, but also intelligent and kind.

It was a winning combination if he'd ever seen one.

Jonah couldn't believe she'd been okay with him coming to work with her. But it had been her idea. He'd fully expected her to insist that he stay outside in the parking lot. If someone at the company was involved, he wanted to be close in case anything went down.

Since they'd arrived, Rachel had been plugging away at her computer, trying to get caught up on some projects. But Jonah knew she was also looking into Draco as she did so. From what he understood, she hadn't found a link to the name yet.

Then again, they'd only been here less than two hours.

Jonah had already talked to Roman. He'd called to check on Rachel. Jonah assured him she was safe.

Then Jonah had called Gage to see if there were any updates on Amar's whereabouts. His friend was supposed to get back with him.

Unfortunately, they didn't have much time.

Jonah knew what he'd seen. And he knew something was going on here on Lantern Beach.

His first priority was keeping Rachel safe, and he was glad he could do that. But another part of him hated standing on the sidelines right now. He wanted to do the investigating while Rachel was tucked away safe somewhere.

Thankfully, no one had treated Rachel strangely when she came in. Dr. Hensley must have kept his word and remained mum about what happened last night. That was a relief, at least.

Jonah had seen William Morey when he went to get some water from the vending machine. Maybe it was Jonah's imagination, but the man almost appeared nervous with his dewy skin and flittering gaze. The bandage on his hand reminded Jonah that the man was hiding something.

Jonah needed to keep an eye on him.

Rachel glanced up at him as she sat behind her desk, and she must have noticed him staring.

A smile spread across her lips. "What are you thinking?"

*About how beautiful you are.* But Jonah didn't dare say that out loud.

"I'm hoping we can find answers soon," he said instead.

Just then, something slammed into her window.

She gasped and her hand flew over her heart.

A man pressed himself against the window, his face distorting as it flattened against the glass. He stared at them, his eyes wide and his pupils dilated. Foam came from his mouth, and he clawed the window as if desperate to get inside.

"Help . . ." the man muttered, the word slurred. "Please, help me!"

Rachel stared at the man with alarm.

This guy had used some of that lotion, hadn't he?

But what was he doing at her window?

The next instant, someone came running around the corner and tackled him.

It must be one of the guards stationed outside.

The men grunted and moaned as they tussled, rising to their feet only to fall again.

"We need you. Now," Jonah said into his phone. Then he shoved it in his pocket. "The police are on their way."

"Thank goodness."

He stepped closer and wrapped his arm around her shoulders. "That was unexpected."

"What's going on?" Rachel stared out the window, halfway expecting the man to have some type of superhuman strength and pop back up.

But he didn't. Not yet.

Rachel heard her coworkers beyond her office door. They'd obviously caught wind of what was happening and were watching also.

The police arrived five minutes later.

As the man was apprehended and put in the back of a squad car, Rachel and Jonah wandered outside.

Cassidy frowned as she paused in front of them. "This just keeps getting better and better, doesn't it?"

"Something like that," Rachel muttered.

"Listen." Cassidy lowered her voice and stepped closer. "Something happened on the island this morning, and I'm trying to figure out if there's any connection to this incident and everything else going on here in Lantern Beach."

"What happened?" Rachel could hardly breathe as she waited for Cassidy to respond.

Cassidy pulled out her phone and hit the screen. Then she showed a photo to Rachel. "Do you recognize this man?"

Rachel's head began to swim.

"I do. That's Santino Lopez."

IN RACHEL'S OFFICE, Jonah and Rachel explained last night's events to Cassidy, starting from when they'd walked into Rachel's house and found Santino sitting in her living room.

They detailed what he'd told them—about the facility in Arizona. About his concerns over the clinical trials. About the nomadic type of people they were using for these trials.

But they really drove home the point when they explained the symptoms some of these people were displaying—symptoms like losing their minds and acting crazy.

And the dead body he'd discovered in the desert.

"Why didn't you contact me as soon as you learned this?" Cassidy's hard gaze flicked between Jonah and Rachel.

"We were still trying to make sense of things," Rachel said. "To sort fact from fiction."

Cassidy crossed her arms and leaned back, clearly deep in thought. "I can't stay quiet about this. I need to bring in help—people who have more resources than I do. My gut tells me that whatever is going on is a serious threat to this community—maybe even beyond this island."

Jonah couldn't disagree with what she'd said. If people's lives were at risk right now, they needed to do something.

"I got the initial tox screen back on those people I arrested here in Lantern Beach . . ." Cassidy began. "There were no signs of the most common drugs, but they're going to do some more testing. However, I did get some additional blood work."

"And?" Rachel leaned forward.

"They appear to have some kind of infection."

"Infection?" Rachel flinched. "What sense does that make?"

"I don't know, but antibiotics aren't helping. Everyone is still being treated and held at the hospital, and their symptoms haven't improved."

"I don't like the sound of that . . ." Rachel's expression tightened.

Cassidy picked up her phone and began calling people. She promised to look into that Arizona facility as well. Maybe she would have more luck than they had.

Jonah hoped and prayed that things didn't get worse before they got better.

But it felt like something had been set in motion, something like an out-of-control train—a danger that would take a mountain to stop.

———

An hour later, a situation room had been set up at the police station.

Rachel, Jonah, Dr. Hensley, and Cassidy had all gathered to formulate a plan. Meanwhile, someone from the FDA as well as two members of the FBI were on their way.

"Let me get this straight." Dr. Hensley leaned on the conference table, his usual intense look in his gaze "You think this all goes back to Natural Defiance, an anti-aging lotion . . . ?"

"That's correct." Cassidy nodded from the front of the table. "That's the only thing that explains what's going on."

"Who would do this?" Rachel shook her head, flabbergasted. "All our products go through rigorous testing."

"Who's been working on this specific project?"

Cassidy's gaze traveled from Rachel back to Dr. Hensley.

Dr. Hensley thought for a moment before listing off the people on that team that developed Natural Defiance.

"But really, anyone at the office could have the ability to do this," Rachel muttered. "Plus, we have to consider the process our products go through. We create the formula, it goes to a production facility where it's manufactured, and afterward it goes through quality control. After it's produced at the plant, then it goes to distributors, then it's transported to stores across the country. There are a lot of steps involved in that—a lot of checks and balances."

"Whoever is behind this is clearly smart." Cassidy tapped a finger on the table in thought. Then she turned to Hensley. "Do you know anything about any production facility affiliated with Ocean Essence in Arizona?"

"In Arizona?" His eyebrows shot up. "No, we don't have any offices or facilities there. Why do you ask?"

"Just curious." She tapped her finger on the table again. "I'm going to need to talk to a few people at this company and see if we can figure out what is going on."

"I already told all my employees they need to stay in the building." Dr. Hensley sat ramrod straight. "I hope all is well in the office and that everyone is cooperating."

"I heard they are," Cassidy said.

Rachel's heart raced.

This was worse than she'd ever even imagined.

"The good news is that it seems to be isolated to the island . . . good news in a very general sense, at least." Cassidy shrugged. "Don't get me wrong—I don't want this happening on Lantern Beach. Not on my watch."

"Me neither," Rachel murmured.

She only hoped they could find some answers before it was too late, and more people were hurt.

# CHAPTER
# TWENTY-NINE

CASSIDY WANTED to talk to each of the employees at Ocean Essence herself. But before she could, the feds arrived at the police station. As she expected, they took over the investigation and issued a recall of Natural Defiance.

However, their presence on the island didn't mean Cassidy would sit back and do nothing.

While the FBI questioned everyone at the cosmetics company, Cassidy called Mac MacArthur, the town mayor and former police chief. He needed to be involved in this.

He arrived less than five minutes later and met with everyone remaining in the station.

"We've got to figure out how we're going to handle this." Cassidy stood at the front of the table, her weariness at war with her adrenaline surge. "If something is going on here, we need to know. If people on this island are in danger, we need to protect them."

The phone in her office continued to ring off the hook.

She had two officers answering calls, and she'd also brought in three Blackout agents to help. Gunner, her new officer in training, was pitching in. She needed to be out there on the streets herself, but she needed to be in here more.

They needed to figure out a solution to what was going on. But all across the island, people were exhibiting the same symptoms. They were acting as if they were out of their minds.

"Chief, I found out something." Officer Leggott paused in her office doorway.

"What's that?"

"The man who delivered the lotion to Lantern Beach—Rachel called with his name."

"Okay . . ."

"His name is Todd Barker. He lives outside of Raleigh." Dillinger shifted. "Anyway, I put in a call to a friend in the area and asked him to check the man out. They had a long talk, and Todd finally admitted he was paid off to deliver an alternate box of products from Ocean Essence to Lantern Beach."

She straightened. "By whom?"

Dillinger shook his head. "He said it was all done

through texts. The box was left outside his house with the lotion and cash payment inside. He never saw anyone."

Her jaw tightened. "I don't like the sound of that."

"Neither do I."

# CHAPTER
# THIRTY

RACHEL RUBBED HER ARMS, still chilled as she thought about the reality of what was happening.

Her mind raced. She needed to figure out some answers before time ran out and more people were hurt—or worse.

She didn't want to think like that. But she had no other choice.

This had to be bigger than just someone at the lab. More than one person had to be involved in order to make this happen.

"Why would someone want to infect people here on an island?" Rachel murmured before glancing at Cassidy. "Have there been reports of this happening anywhere else?"

"Not that I've heard. I've been keeping my eyes open and asking around."

"It just doesn't make sense." Rachel shook her head and frowned as she felt a headache coming on. "I just can't figure out the person's motive for doing this."

"The most common motives people have are love, money, and power."

"I can't see how love would be involved in this," Rachel said. "Nor can I see how someone would profit off of making people act crazy or even how this could make someone feel more powerful. There's something we're missing."

"You're right. There is more to this." Cassidy glanced at her phone again, and her expression tightened.

"What is it?" Rachel leaned closer, anxious to hear what she had to say.

"In the past two hours, the police station has had thirty-two calls about people acting peculiar. The clinic is overrun with people going in with similar symptoms. I have a feeling it's only going to get worse from here."

"You may be right." Jonah's cheek flickered as if he fought a frown. "We don't have any time to waste in trying to find these answers."

"I already called Ty. He's taking Faith to his parents, and he told them to lock their doors and to be careful. Some people are just acting crazy, but others are turning violent. Unlike drugs, this doesn't seem to be wearing off. Then, he's on his way here to help."

Cassidy's phone rang again, and she sounded grim as she answered.

When she ended the call, she turned back toward them. "That was the FBI. They're locking down this island until they have more answers. No one can come and no one can go."

Rachel let those words settle in her mind.

This was turning into something from her worst nightmares.

# CHAPTER
# THIRTY-ONE

JONAH LISTENED to everything taking place around him at the police station and tried to comprehend it all.

Mac and Cassidy were working on letting islanders know what was going on. Lantern Beach had an emergency alert system set up that officials were utilizing now. The automated system would send out both texts and phone calls to locals, notifying them that the island was on lockdown. People had been asked to bring any bottles of Natural Defiance to the police station, and they already had two boxes full of the product.

Dr. Hensley also remained in the situation room. He studied Ocean Essence's finances as well as the employee logs. He had background checks for every employee, but he was going to review that paperwork as well.

Rachel was researching the lab results of that lotion she'd gotten earlier.

And Jonah was here to watch over Rachel and make sure she remained safe.

The phone at the police station continued to ring of the hook as more calls came in.

The whole place felt like a zoo—and Jonah couldn't ignore the desperation in the air.

He also couldn't ignore how exhausted Rachel looked. She was carrying this as her personal responsibility, wasn't she?

Knowing her, she was.

Jonah had wanted to protect her. But what if by coming here he'd only brought more trouble?

His heart knotted at the thought of it.

The door opened, and Jonah glanced up.

Officer Leggott staggered inside.

As soon as Jonah saw the man's dilated pupils and jerky movements, he braced himself.

Had the officer used that lotion too?

No . . .

Jonah rose to his feet.

"Leggott . . ." Cassidy muttered.

Before anyone could make a move, Leggott charged into the room, his arms flailing and drool coming from his mouth.

He went right toward Cassidy.

Before he reached her, Mac grabbed one of his arms and Jonah the other.

But the man seemed to have almost superhuman strength. He tried to toss them away, reminding Jonah of the Bible story of Legion, the demon-possessed man Jesus healed.

Jonah and Mac held him in place until Cassidy put handcuffs on his wrists. Leggott struggled against her every move.

"I . . . can't . . . control . . . myself . . ." Leggott muttered.

"Then we'll help you," Cassidy said, snapping the cuffs in place. "Sorry to have to do this, but it's for your own good."

Once he was subdued, Jonah and Mac kept a tight grip on him.

Cassidy straightened and caught her breath. Her lips were pulled into a grim line, and hair escaped her bun.

Subduing her officer had knocked the wind from her lungs, hadn't it?

"Take him to the holding cell for now." Cassidy's voice held no nonsense. "We need to do it for our safety as well as for his."

Rachel's heart still raced from each turn of events.

Ten minutes had passed since Officer Leggott had come into the situation room acting out of his mind. Now, he was in a holding cell. The island clinic was at capacity, and a space was being set up at the local elementary school to accommodate more people who had been infected.

The cases were multiplying quickly—too quickly for the limited number of people on this island to keep up with it.

Her adrenaline pumped as she remembered the sight of the normally easy-going man.

This combination of toxic algae and jimsonweed could turn the best of people into monsters.

That was exactly what someone wanted, wasn't it?

Someone wanted to transform this whole island into a place of chaos, disorder, and danger.

She felt sick at the thought of it.

This had to be bigger than one person being mad at someone on the island or being upset about something that had happened here. There were larger implications at play.

"What are you thinking?" Cassidy stared at Rachel from across the table.

She decided not to sugarcoat her words. "This is bigger than that lotion. All these people couldn't be using Natural Defiance. There's no possible way.

Besides, Leggott would have known better than to touch the stuff."

"What's your theory?" Jonah took another sip of coffee as he studied her.

"I think Velocity is a cover organization, and someone put my name on that clinical trial so I could take the fall if things went south."

"Keep going." Cassidy narrowed her eyes as she listened closely.

"I think that lotion was just a test, and once someone saw how people reacted after using it, whoever is behind this decided to move onto a more commonly used substance instead so it could have a greater effect."

"What would that be?" Jonah shifted as he waited for her answer.

"What *could* it be?" Rachel's thoughts continued to race, and she tapped her finger against her lips. "What's a substance that most of the people here on the island might use?"

"Sunscreen?" Mac suggested.

"I saw someone giving out samples of a new shampoo the other day," Hensley said with a shrug. "But it wasn't an Ocean Essence product."

None of those things sounded quite right.

They all knew it.

Jonah stood. He grabbed a paper cup from the

dispenser and walked to the water fountain in the corner to refill it.

That was when a realization hit her.

The water.

Not the water from a swimming pool or hot tub.

But water that everyone on the island used.

Rachel darted across the room and smacked the cup out of his hands.

The cup clattered on the floor as liquid splashed at his feet.

"What are you doing?" The way Jonah looked at her made it clear that he wondered if Rachel had been infected and gone crazy also.

"It's the water," she rushed. "It's the only thing that makes sense. Someone has infected the water here on the island."

Silence stretched through the room as everyone let that thought settle.

# CHAPTER
# THIRTY-TWO



The feds were currently testing the island's water.

Thankfully, the FBI realized the seriousness of this situation and were pouring major resources and manpower into finding answers. Jonah hoped they would know something soon.

Another alert had gone out to the town to inform people that the drinking water may be unsafe. Locals and tourists had also been warned to not consume it or use it to wash their hands or dishes or to shower—not until something more definitive could be confirmed.

Dr. Hensley and Rachel had both emphasized the fact that the skin was the largest organ and how if there was something in the water, it could be transferred through skin contact.

That would make targeting the town's water supply the best way to spread this toxic chemical combination to the most people by the quickest means. Someone would have had to dump large quantities into the water—and somehow, they'd figured out how to do it.

Rachel stared at the window, lines of worry across her forehead. "Why would someone do this? We need to figure out a motive."

That was when the realization hit him.

Jonah straightened, almost not wanting to voice his theory out loud. Yet he couldn't keep it to himself either.

"Biological warfare," Jonah announced.

"Biological warfare?" Rachel's voice came out wispy as she turned toward him with wide eyes.

"It makes sense." His thoughts rushed until they formed a formidable—and likely—theory in his mind. "This island is the perfect place for phase two of these clinical trials. Maybe they even chose this location to rub it in the face of Ocean Essence. It's the ultimate gesture of disrespect. If the wrong person got their hands on a formula that could make people act crazy, then they might try to use it against countries they consider their enemies."

Silence spread through the room again as everyone comprehended that idea.

But no one argued. They knew he was correct. It was the only thing that made sense.

"I think you're right." Cassidy nodded slowly. "Maybe this formula was even developed by accident, and someone at the lab took it upon themselves to sell this mix-up to the highest bidder—an enemy of the US."

Jonah didn't like the sound of that.

"We need motive." Cassidy crossed her arms as she glanced at each person in the room. "Who would want to do this and why? For the money?"

"I'd almost think it has to be someone who's angry with either Lantern Beach or the people here," Jonah said. "I mean, why else target the island?"

"Good point." Rachel nodded. "This feels personal, doesn't it? But for all we know, it could be someone targeting Ocean Essence or even Blackout."

"It could . . ." Cassidy tapped her lips. "But I don't think that's it." She glanced at Rachel. "What about William? Does he have any reason to hate this island?"

Rachel thought about it a moment before shaking her head. "Not that I can think of."

Jonah couldn't stop thinking about one of his assignments back when he'd been part of the secret government program.

He remembered Amar Ravish and his men. Larchmont had intel that they were on US soil.

What if that really was Ravish that Jonah had seen on Lantern Beach?

What if the man had discovered Jonah had been here? If he'd discovered Jonah's connection with Rachel and the fact she worked for Ocean Essence?

Could Ravish hate Jonah enough to use various parts of his life against him?

He wouldn't put it past the guy and his men.

They hated America . . . and they hated Jonah for killing their second-in-command—Amar's brother.

If that was true, then who did these men have on their payroll here in Lantern Beach? At Ocean Essence?

Jonah needed to find out.

Now.

———

It was a race to determine who was responsible, and Rachel felt the pressure mounting.

As the group remained in the situation room, they all brainstormed who might be responsible.

In the meantime, the National Guard was on their way. They were bringing clean water that residents and tourists could use until everything was sorted out.

Right now, Cassidy and her team's first priority was bringing in William Morey.

He made the most sense to question.

Cassidy had already sent Officer Dillinger to William's house to pick him up.

Maybe William would provide some answers.

But every minute that passed felt more like an hour, Rachel mused. Her head pounded, her back ached, and her muscles were so tense she felt as if they might snap.

The pressure of the situation was clearly getting to her.

Finally, Dillinger stepped into the room—alone. Based on his frown, he didn't have good news.

"I went to William's place." He rubbed his jaw before continuing. "He wasn't there. I tried to call. He didn't answer. He's not at the lab either."

Rachel massaged the skin between her eyes. She shouldn't be surprised. Yet she'd been hopeful . . .

But here they were with yet another roadblock.

"There's more," Dillinger said. "I found some lab equipment in his house."

"Lab equipment?" Rachel asked. "What kind?"

"I don't know enough to tell you that. A microscope and some test tubes. Seemed kind of weird for him to have those things at his house."

"I'd say," Rachel said.

"Also, I found his cell phone on the bedroom floor inside his house. There were several missed text messages on his screen that I could preview.

Someone told him that this was all over and that he should get out of town before everything hit the fan."

Rachel frowned.

If that didn't sound like guilt, she didn't know what did . . .

# CHAPTER
# THIRTY-THREE

JONAH'S THOUGHTS raced as he mentally reviewed what Dillinger had shared.

His assignments with the Shadow Agency were top secret.

*Beyond* top secret.

They were off the books.

Even when he'd been in the military, he'd been told if he was caught or apprehended while executing his assignments that the United States would disavow themselves from him and claim ignorance.

That was because Jonah didn't really exist on paper.

That made him disposable.

The thought hadn't used to bother him. He'd

figured someone had to take one for the team—the team being the United States.

Jonah had been that person.

But something was beginning to change inside him.

Rachel had made him realize there was more to life than he'd thought.

Now he never wanted to go back to what his life had been.

Maybe he *did* deserve a chance at stability.

At love.

He glanced at Rachel again. Saw the lines of concern across her forehead. Saw the tight set of her mouth. The tension in her shoulders.

That was when he made his decision.

He was tired of playing by other people's rules.

His spine straightened as he turned to everyone around him. "I thought I saw Amar Ravish on the island."

Each person at the table turned toward him.

"Ravish . . . the terrorist?" Cassidy bristled as she said the words.

Jonah nodded solemnly. "Yes, he's the one."

Rachel leaned closer. "He's the one you made mad? One of the FBI's top ten most wanted? The man who dropped bombs on airports across Europe to assert his dominance?"

Jonah nodded again. "My team and I took the life

of his right-hand man, who happened to also be his brother. Amar has been bent on revenge ever since. Has been trying to track us down. However, my team all had code names to keep ourselves safe. Recently, I've feared he discovered our true identities. Two members of the team were nearly killed. One is currently in the hospital in ICU after a bullet lodged dangerously close to his heart."

Cassidy stared at him another moment, something close to disbelief in her gaze, before asking, "When did you think you saw him? And why didn't you mention this earlier?"

Jonah swallowed hard before launching into the truth. He couldn't keep this to himself any longer. "It's top secret, and I'll probably be fired for mentioning it to you now. But I can't help but wonder if he may have something to do with what's going on here on the island."

"You think he'd tamper with the water system?" Mac's eyes narrowed as he seemed to calculate a plan for how to tackle this.

The man was spry and smart. Not only that, but he clearly loved this island and wanted more than anything to protect it.

"I think if he could hurt me while enacting his plan to destroy America as we know it . . . then yes," Jonah said. "He's an evil man."

"But . . . to contaminate the entire water system

on an island . . ." Rachel frowned, a pinched look on her face. "It would take so much product to taint that quantity of water. I'm talking truckloads and truckloads. Certainly someone would notice that. It's not something that could be done under the radar."

Cassidy let out a breath and stood. "I'm going to need to share this update with the FBI."

"Do what you have to do." Jonah nodded. "In the meantime, I need to make some calls to my colleagues. Maybe they know something they haven't shared."

"Who exactly do you work for?" Cassidy paused before moving.

"I'll tell you. But not right now. It will take too long to explain, and time isn't something we have."

Cassidy stared at him another moment before nodding, seeming to agree with his words. "Okay then. Let's get busy."

———

An hour later, William still hadn't been found, and Rachel felt as if she were on pins and needles.

Food had been brought in—sandwiches safely prepared at The Crazy Chefette. Bottled water had also been left, along with some chips and some bottled cold brew coffee from the store.

They were all going to need their energy if they

were going to find answers. Daylight hours were fading fast.

"Either William Morey is hiding out or he's been taken out," Jonah announced, tapping a potato chip against his paper plate.

"Agreed," Cassidy said. "Hopefully, we'll have some answers soon."

"What do we do until then?" Rachel asked.

Cassidy's lips pulled into a tight line until she said, "The FBI is at our water treatment facility right now. But I'd like to put my eyes on the place myself. I just can't stay here and not do anything."

"I'd like to go with you." Rachel rose.

"I'm not sure that's a good idea." Cassidy pressed her lips together and twisted her head with hesitation.

"If they did something to the water, I'm your best chance at figuring out what it is. I can use my skills and knowledge to help." The way Rachel said the words left no room for doubt. She knew what her abilities were, and she wasn't going to shrink away. "I do have two PhDs."

Cassidy stared at her another moment before nodding slowly. "Okay then. Come with me. You can probably ask the right questions to those in charge or maybe even examine some readings."

Jonah rose also. "And me?"

"You stay here and keep trying to get up with

your friends," Cassidy said. "We need any information they may be able to provide. Don't worry—I'll take good care of Rachel."

Jonah hesitated a moment almost as if he wanted to argue. Instead, he nodded.

He had to know Rachel was in good hands with Cassidy. Yet Rachel also knew that he was protective of her.

A few minutes later, she and Cassidy departed.

Rachel's nerves thrummed inside her as they headed down the road.

What would they discover?

Whatever it was, having answers was better than not knowing. At least if they had answers, they could figure out a solution.

Facing the truth was hard, but it was always the best choice.

When they pulled up to the plant, three FBI sedans were already there.

"This could be hairy," Cassidy muttered as she stared at the scene. "The FBI can be territorial. I'll handle these guys."

They climbed out and started toward the front of the building. Before they even reached the doors, a man stepped out.

"That's Larry Haley," Cassidy told Rachel. "He's a supervisor here."

Rachel observed the man a moment. He appeared

to be in his fifties, with a deep tan on his face and even deeper wrinkles. His long, sun-bleached hair had been pulled into a ponytail. A surfer, if she had to guess.

When he saw Cassidy, he rushed toward her. Worry stretched through his gaze.

"Chief Chambers . . ." he started. "We have another problem."

Cassidy gripped his arm. "What's wrong?"

"It's Derek . . ."

"Derek Dawson?" Cassidy stared at him.

He nodded quickly, his shoulders tight and his words clipped. "He didn't come in today. I've been trying to call him. He's not answering."

"What exactly is his job here?" Cassidy asked.

His gaze locked with Cassidy's. "Quality control."

Rachel pressed her eyes closed.

Two missing people.

Two missing people who might have the answers they need.

That couldn't be a coincidence.

Everything was reaching a boiling point . . . and soon that dangerous water would spill over and cause unthinkable damage to anyone close.

FBI AGENT BROWNSTONE took over the situation.

He remained at the police headquarters, doling out instructions to other FBI agents and the Lantern Beach PD.

While Cassidy and Rachel were gone, Brownstone came into the conference room. The man was in his forties and brisk, looking more office smart than tough. But his brown eyes were sharp and perceptive.

Jonah was reserving his opinion on the man until he saw him in action.

Brownstone gathered everyone's attention and gave them an update on the situation—which wasn't much.

"I don't feel confident that the emergency text

messages are getting to the tourists as they should be," Brownstone said. "We're going to need to establish teams to go door to door and let people know what's going on."

Jonah could see his point. Locals were on the alert system. But people renting houses might not get the message from owners or management companies.

Brownstone shifted in front of them. "Even though the National Guard is here, and they can help, I'd like some volunteers also. I'd particularly like volunteers who have military or law enforcement training. I've already talked to the guys at Blackout, and they've agreed to help."

"I can help too." Jonah raised a hand as he sat at the conference table. "I'm former US military."

"Very well. We're going to meet outside and divide up search areas. A grid system is already in place, thanks to Mayor MacArthur." Agent Brownstone nodded at Mac. "We have no time to waste right now. Let's gather everyone outside. Whatever you do, don't drink, touch, or even think about using this island's water. Understand?"

Everyone agreed.

Jonah wished Rachel was back so he could talk to her before he left to scour the island.

But the meeting only took about twenty minutes and then everybody was off.

Jonah would take a section of houses near the boardwalk.

He drove there and parked in a nearby lot before beginning his rounds.

But he paused when he saw a crowd gathered on the boardwalk near someone selling popcorn and pretzels.

A familiar face caught his eye.

Was that . . . Larchmont?

Was his boss here on the island?

If so, how long had he been here?

The man couldn't have arrived within the past several hours. He had to have come before the island was locked down.

Jonah's muscles tightened as more questions collided in his head.

———

Rachel and Cassidy headed toward Derek's house to talk to him.

She had a feeling he wouldn't be there.

Was Derek involved with this situation? Had he and William worked together?

Rachel had a feeling that, even if that was the case, someone else was acting as the puppet master and pulling the strings.

Could it be Amar Ravish?

There was a good chance of it.

The whole situation felt like a nightmare.

As they'd traveled, Cassidy talked back and forth on her radio, and they learned that the FBI had put together teams to talk to people on the island, to warn them about the dangers, and to answer any questions.

Rachel had a feeling Cassidy didn't like someone stepping on her toes. But in this situation, she didn't have much choice.

A few minutes later, Rachel and Cassidy pulled up to Derek's cottage, which was located on the sound side of the island.

She and Rachel walked together toward Derek's door, and Cassidy knocked.

There was no answer.

She waited a few minutes before knocking again. "Derek, Police Chief Cassidy Chambers. We need to talk to you."

There was a car outside—according to Cassidy, a vehicle that was registered to Derek.

There was still no answer.

As Rachel lingered near the door, Cassidy paced the perimeter and tried to peer in the windows.

"The blinds are drawn. I'm going to have to go in." Cassidy drew in a deep breath before bracing herself. "Stand back."

Cassidy then kicked the door. The wood around the facing splintered.

Three kicks later, the door swung open.

If the situation weren't so tenuous, Rachel might be impressed.

Cassidy straightened as she stared inside the open doorway. "Stay there."

She drew her gun and cautiously stepped inside.

Rachel held her breath as she wondered what the police chief might find.

# CHAPTER
# THIRTY-FIVE

AS SOON AS Larchmont realized he'd been spotted, he darted away.

But Jonah wasn't going to let him get away from this so easily.

Jonah took off after his boss. The fact he was trying to hide only made Larchmont look guilty.

When Jonah reached an alley between two shops, he froze.

Larchmont was there.

Waiting for him.

The man was tall with a shock of white hair and distinguished features that masked the fact he was a trained assassin—someone who'd been taught to think strictly with logic and set aside any emotion.

That had served him well in his career.

But on a personal level, it had been detrimental.

Tension spread across Jonah's muscles as he cautiously stepped toward the man. "What are you doing here?"

"I needed to talk to you face-to-face."

Jonah bristled as he paused in front of him. "Funny, it doesn't seem like you're trying to talk to me. It seems like you're spying on me. Or maybe you have something to do with what's going on here."

Larchmont's gaze darkened. "It's not like that."

"Then why are you here? When did you arrive?"

"I just got here this morning before all this craziness happened. I was going to find you, but I was waiting for the right opportunity."

"Why did you want to 'talk to me face-to-face'?" Jonah put air quotes around the words since Larchmont hadn't even indicated to Jonah that he was coming.

"We got word that a terrorist attack is being planned. This island was thrown out as a possible location. I don't know if Amar has anything to do with it or not, but I wanted to warn you in person. I see that I might be too late."

CASSIDY REAPPEARED in the doorway less than five minutes later.

Rachel stared up at the police chief, noting her grim expression.

She'd found something, and it wasn't good. Rachel had no doubt about that.

"Derek is inside." Cassidy slid her phone into her pocket, and her gun had been holstered. "He's dead."

Rachel gasped. "Murdered?"

Her frown deepened. "If I had to guess based on the angle of the gunshot wound, it's suicide. We'll investigate more thoroughly, however."

"Was there a note?" Rachel asked.

Cassidy shook her head. "No, there wasn't."

"Maybe he couldn't take the guilt over what he'd

done." Rachel wrapped her arms across her chest, more and more tension causing her muscles to ache.

"Maybe. I just called my guys, and they're on the way. I want to hold tight until they arrive to secure the scene. Then I want to go to the lab."

"Ocean Essence?" Rachel's eyebrows shot up with surprise.

"Yes, I'd like for you to test the island's water yourself."

"Isn't the FBI doing that?"

"They are. But I want my own results. Plus, I have a feeling you'll be faster."

"Whatever you need," Rachel said.

She didn't want to show her excitement over Cassidy's suggestion. But Rachel desperately wanted to know what might be in the water also.

Maybe they'd have some answers soon.

———

Rachel pulled her safety goggles off and pushed herself away from the microscope.

She turned toward Cassidy, who stood behind her in the lab. "It's just as I suspected. Someone laced the island's water with algae, jimsonweed, and some type of bacteria as well. But there's more than that. I believe the jimsonweed was synthesized, which only made its effects stronger."

"How so?" Cassidy narrowed her eyes.

"I believe it also makes people highly suggestive. That would explain the man who showed up on my doorstep at my house and the one at my office window. Someone may have told them to do that in order to frighten me."

Cassidy's gaze darkened. "And how long will these effects last?"

"That's a good question. If they laced it with a bacterium, then it could stay in a person's system . . ." She shrugged. "It depends if it's an acute or chronic bacterial infection. If it's acute and not treated with antibiotics, it could stay in someone's system for a couple of weeks. If it's chronic, then longer."

"Why would they add a bacterium?"

Rachel nibbled on her lip a moment. "I wish I knew, but I don't. It doesn't make a lot of sense unless someone wanted these effects to be lasting. I'm still trying to figure out what type of bacterium this is exactly."

Silence stretched out the moments.

Finally, Rachel said, "The one thing I know for sure is that, if this was all done on purpose, it's definitely an act of terrorism."

Cassidy frowned and crossed her arms with a sigh. "That's what I was afraid you were going to say. I'll give your results to the FBI, even though I'm sure they already have their own results. I like to do my own research."

The way she said the words made Rachel wonder if she couldn't always trust that the feds would share pertinent information with her. She could understand Cassidy's hesitation. When more than one law enforcement agency was involved, things no doubt got complicated.

"What now?" Rachel turned toward Cassidy, her thoughts thrumming.

"We need to keep working to figure out who did this. I know Derek wasn't acting on his own."

Rachel agreed with her assessment. "No word on William?"

"No, it's like he disappeared off the face of the earth."

Theories tried to form in Rachel's mind, but she stopped them. She didn't have enough information yet to draw any conclusions, and she didn't want to muddy her thinking. Plus, finding William may not give them the answers they were seeking. Right now, they had to figure out how to stop this.

"Let's get back to the police station and see if there are any updates." Cassidy took a step toward the door.

Before they left the lab, Cassidy's radio buzzed.

It was Officer Dillinger.

A body had been found in the Pamlico Sound.
The body of William Morey.

# CHAPTER
# THIRTY-SEVEN

JONAH STILL FELT apprehensive as he made his way back to the police station after talking to Larchmont. He'd quickly visited the houses on his part of the grid to warn residents, visitors, and property owners of what was going on.

It had taken an hour—and that was just the amount of time he needed to think this through.

Relief filled him when he spotted Rachel stretching her legs in the conference room. Without hesitation, he pulled her into his arms.

She didn't resist.

"I'm glad you're okay," he whispered in her ear.

She nestled beneath his chin. "You too."

He wished they could stay this way. But they couldn't. Too much was on the line, and they all needed to share their notes right now.

Jonah didn't plan on keeping it a secret that Larchmont was here.

He was, however, shocked to hear William Morey was dead.

The man had been shot and then dumped into the water.

Whoever was behind this—Amar Ravish, he assumed—would stop at nothing to get what they wanted.

Lantern Beach was the perfect testing ground for what could be a bigger plan to take down this country as they knew it.

They all gathered and shared their information. The meeting was relatively short, however.

It was already dark outside now, and it had been a long day.

"Essential personnel need to stay here and keep searching for information," Agent Brownstone told the group. "I suggest the rest of you try to get some sleep, and then tomorrow we meet back here. We'll keep trying to figure this out."

"How long are you going to keep people corralled on the island?" Cassidy stared at Brownstone, just daring him to keep her out of the loop.

Brownstone's expression remained hard and unyielding. "Until we know who is behind this."

"Do you think it's contagious?" Rachel asked.

"We don't know anything right now."

"I don't believe this is a virus, but a bacterial infection could also be contagious."

"Exactly." His gaze darkened. "We need more proof than that before we make any calls. This is now a matter of national security. We have the Coast Guard monitoring the shores to make sure no one tries to leave by boat or by other means. If they do, the fines will be hefty, and it will be considered a criminal act."

His words drove home the seriousness of this situation.

Jonah, for one, wanted to stay here at the meeting.

But when he glanced at Rachel and saw the exhaustion beneath her eyes, his thoughts shifted.

She needed to rest. This had been a lot on her.

Even though his first inclination was to stay awake all night until he found answers, sleep deprivation would catch up with them quickly.

He should let the FBI do their jobs and then join them again in the morning.

Now he just needed to convince Rachel of that.

———

Jonah had insisted to Rachel that she go home and rest, and she'd begrudgingly agreed.

There was really nothing else she could do here

right now. She'd tested those water samples and given her input.

Rachel knew if she left that Jonah would also go because he wouldn't leave her alone with everything going on.

She found comfort in knowing he'd be close. She also found comfort in knowing her dad wasn't here on the island. He wouldn't be able to get back to Lantern Beach either.

A few minutes later, they walked into the house, and Rachel dropped her purse by the door before plopping on the couch.

Her brain was a strange mix of wound-up and exhausted.

Jonah lowered himself beside her, concern laced in his gaze.

"I know this has been a lot for you," he said softly.

She shrugged. "It's been a lot for all of us, hasn't it?"

"I'm sorry you've been pulled into the middle of this." His voice dropped to a lower, more intimate tone.

"You really think that Amar is behind this?" She studied his gaze.

"He's the only one that makes sense. The question is who else does he have working for him?"

She stared off into the distance in thought before

looking at him again. "Your boss really showed up in Lantern Beach?"

He nodded. "He has intel that an unknown group of terrorists may be planning something here in Lantern Beach. He came here himself to warn me."

"Why not just call?"

"He's a master spy. He doesn't always trust talking on the phone. Plus, he probably wanted to check out what I was up to before contacting me. When you live like he has, you learn not to trust anyone."

"It sounds like a horrible way to live."

Jonah shrugged. "I know a little about living like that, and it is."

Rachel pressed her eyes closed as exhaustion continued to wash over her. She wanted to keep pushing forward. To solve problems. To do something.

But she was both physically and mentally exhausted.

"Hey, come here . . ." Jonah wrapped his arm behind her.

Before she could question herself, she fell into his arms.

She'd always felt safe there.

She stayed nestled against his chest, making no move to sit up. The steady beat of his heart and the familiar scent of his aftershave brought her waves of comfort.

But she probably shouldn't be doing this. She was only going to end up getting her heart broken again. Could she really afford to let that happen?

She lifted her head, wishing she didn't have to have this conversation.

Her gaze caught with Jonah's, and she saw the emotions swirling in his eyes.

She still loved this man. She knew she did.

But now she wondered if maybe he loved her too.

The thought both thrilled and terrified her.

# THIRTY-EIGHT

JONAH STARED into Rachel's eyes and felt his heart quicken.

He gently pushed a lock of hair behind her ear and left his hand to rest on her cheek.

She'd quickly become the most important person in his life, and he'd been a fool to let her get away. He'd known it from the moment he'd left, but he'd tried to convince himself it was the right choice.

It hadn't been.

Was it too late to fix things?

He needed to find out.

"Rachel . . ." he murmured.

She gazed up at him unblinking, and her eyes so full of emotions—hope and maybe even some fear. "Yes?"

"I'm sorry." The words came out as a whisper.

"About what?"

"About everything. About pulling you into this. About leaving you. But mostly about being wrong."

She tilted her head. "What were you wrong about?"

He gazed into her eyes. "I should have never broken up with you. I was trying to protect you, and instead I hurt you. The very thing I feared happening happened anyway. Trouble found you even though we weren't dating."

Her shoulders softened, and she licked her lips as her voice took on a throaty tone. "I wish you had told me your fears."

"I was afraid you'd convince me otherwise and that I'd regret it if you got hurt." Everything else—even every thought of the urgency of this situation—seemed to disappear for just a moment.

Rachel gently ran her fingertips across his cheek and jaw. "I'll never fault you for telling me the truth. I like making informed decisions. What I don't like is being taken out of the equation."

"I understand that now. I was a fool to do what I did."

"You were."

A smile spread across Jonah's face. He liked the fact Rachel hadn't denied his words. Because if she had, she would have been lying.

"Besides, I'd rather fight my battles with you than fight without you," Rachel murmured.

As their gazes caught, his breath seemed to freeze.

He gently stroked her cheek.

Then Jonah did what he'd been wanting to do ever since he left Lantern Beach.

He moved closer and leaned toward her.

His face lingered mere inches from Rachel as he asked the silent question: Can I kiss you?

He couldn't mess this up. Not again.

Rachel seemed to stop breathing in front of him, and time froze.

All Jonah could think about was their closeness. About the sweet smell of her cherry-scent lip balm. About her soft skin under his touch. About her silky hair as it brushed his fingers.

The next instant, Rachel wrapped her arms around his neck.

Then she accepted his invitation.

She pressed her lips into his, and pure bliss washed over him.

Just for a moment in the middle of all of the chaos, everything felt right.

He knew the feeling wouldn't last long, but he would enjoy the moment while he could.

Rachel turned in for the evening, but she knew she'd have trouble sleeping.

She couldn't stop thinking about the kiss.

Then, after replaying it in her mind too many times to count, guilt filled her.

She shouldn't be thinking about anything other than the crisis they had on their hands.

After fully reprimanding herself, she tried to run through any information she might have missed.

Yet she knew that sometimes sleeping was the best way to pull those things out of her subconscious. There had been many occasions where she'd been trying to figure out a problem, and all she needed to do was rest. When she awoke, she had the answers that she needed.

She pulled her comforter up higher, her pillow suddenly feeling like a brick beneath her head. She lay in her bed and wondered what life would look like tomorrow. She knew that in the blink of an eye everything could change.

That was what had happened when her mom died. But it had mostly been just her world and her dad's world that had changed. That had been devastating in its own right.

But if someone had their way, then life as people knew it here in the United States could very well transform into something unrecognizable.

Rachel hated to think about it, but she knew it was a reality.

That was why she needed answers.

She sighed and turned over in bed again, trying to put her thoughts to rest.

But her brain kept turning and turning and turning.

Finally, she began to settle down.

Before drifting off, she prayed that rest would bring her answers.

She tried not to fear what tomorrow might hold.

And at some time deep in the night, a restless sleep found her.

EVEN THOUGH JONAH had emphasized to Rachel how important it was that she get some sleep, he wasn't able to sleep himself.

Instead, he remained on his phone talking to different colleagues and trying to figure out if any of them knew of Amar Ravish's whereabouts.

At 1:00 a.m., his phone buzzed.

It was Larchmont.

He said he'd remembered something he wanted to talk to Jonah about—again, face-to-face.

But there was no way that Jonah was leaving Rachel here while he went out to meet his boss.

Instead, he asked Larchmont to come to Rachel's house. Jonah had no doubt the man already knew where Rachel lived. If Jonah knew the man like he thought he did, he'd probably scoped out the place already.

Ten minutes after the phone call, a car pulled into the driveway.

Jonah stepped outside, ready to talk to Larchmont.

There was no need to wake Rachel up for this.

Jonah crossed his arms as his boss got out of the car and walked up to him.

"What's going on?" Jonah demanded.

"I wanted you to be the first to hear." Larchmont paused, drifting to the shadows as he always did.

"Hear what?"

"Some of our guys just confirmed that an arms dealer is planning on testing some type of biological weapon here in this area."

Jonah sucked in a breath. He didn't like the sound of that.

He glanced at Larchmont. "You have to let the FBI know."

Larchmont stepped closer. "The FBI isn't even supposed to know I exist. But if you talk to them, just know . . . . this formula was auctioned to the highest bidder after being accidentally discovered."

"And then the winner opened that lab in Arizona . . ."

"Yes, it was all cloak and dagger. Workers and

participants didn't know what they were getting into."

"And now he's here. To enact the second part of his plan?"

"That's my theory. He plans on doing a lot of damage with his winnings."

Jonah didn't like the sound of that . . .

———

Rachel watched in horror as a vacationer—complete with a farmer's tan—chased another vacationer down the beach with knife in hand.

She had to find the antibiotic that could help these people! They had to regain their right minds.

And the solution was in her hand.

She'd figured out the winning formula.

But as she stared at the bottle, she couldn't remember how she'd done it.

If she wanted to reproduce this antibiotic, she needed to know the formula she'd used . . .

The woman screamed as the man with the knife grabbed her and plunged the weapon into her back.

No . . .

She stared at the bottle, desperation kicking in.

She needed answers! Now!

Just as the words started to clear, she was jostled awake.

She'd just been sleeping.

It had been a nightmare.

Her eyes flung open as dreams and reality crashed around her.

She dragged in several shallow breaths as she tried to calm her racing heart.

It seemed so real. She had been so close to finding answers.

So what had woken her?

She glanced around the room, wondering if it was a sound.

The next instant, a figure in black stepped through her patio door.

A scream caught in her throat.

She'd locked that door. She knew she had.

So how . . . ?

He must have picked the lock.

She started to scream for help.

Before she could, the man pounced on top of her.

Panic rushed through her.

He'd trapped her.

No . . .

In the blink of an eye, he had a cloth in his hands.

He pressed it across her mouth.

She struggled, fought to get the man away from her. Grabbing his wrists, she shoved against him with all her strength.

It did no good.

He was too strong.

As her thoughts began to blur, she glanced up.

And all she could see was his eyes.

Cold, unfamiliar eyes.

Everything around her blurred.

An all-consuming fatigue claimed her.

Her eyes drooped.

Whatever that substance had been on the cloth, it knocked her out completely.

WHEN JONAH STEPPED BACK inside the house, his thoughts remained on what Larchmont had told him.

He was going to need time to process his boss's statements. To figure out how to handle this.

Someone had purchased the formula for the biological weapon. And this person had already begun testing it.

He had to let Rachel know.

He headed up the stairs to Rachel's room and softly knocked at her door. When there was no answer, he twisted the knob.

Jonah fully expected to see Rachel lying in bed snoozing.

Instead, the covers had been thrown back.

Her bed was empty.

He tried to keep his apprehension at bay.

Maybe she was just in the bathroom.

But as he glanced at the open door to the attached bathroom, the inside was dark.

Tension crept through his muscles.

"Rachel?" But no one was there to hear his words.

That was when he noticed the breeze blowing the curtains back from the open sliding patio door.

Rachel was . . . gone.

Someone had taken her.

Had Larchmont's presence here tonight just been a distraction? Was Larchmont working with Amar?

Red-hot fury filled Jonah's veins at the thought.

He rushed to the sliding door and out onto the deck.

He scanned the beach.

There was nothing. No one.

How long had he been outside talking to Larchmont?

Probably twenty minutes.

That was plenty of time for someone to grab Rachel and get her far from here.

Jonah's only comfort was in knowing that they probably hadn't been able to take her off the island. Not with the Coast Guard patrolling it.

If she was still here on Lantern Beach, he would find her . . . if it was the last thing he did.

Jonah grabbed his phone and called Larchmont.

He would demand some answers from the man . . . especially if Jonah had just been set up.

———

When Rachel awoke, she was lying on a gritty floor.

In a dark room with no windows.

She sat up and brushed dirt off her face.

She glanced around, trying to figure out where she was.

But she couldn't see anything.

Her grogginess slowly cleared as she remembered what had happened.

Someone had broken into her home and abducted her.

Bile rose in her throat.

But why had she been taken?

*Where* had she been taken?

Had Amar kidnapped her?

A shudder raced through her at that thought.

If a deadly terrorist had grabbed her, then there was a good chance she wouldn't walk away from this alive.

Had she been abducted just to make Jonah pay? Would they try to force her to do some type of evil deed using her scientific knowledge and skills?

It took some struggling, but she finally managed to pull herself to her feet.

She stepped carefully until she found a wall. Felt along the surface. Trying to find something that would provide her answers as to where she was.

She reached up to gauge the height of the ceiling, and she touched a rafter right above her head. Then felt another.

An attic, she realized.

It seemed everything had been cleared out of the area.

But she felt certain, based on the size of the room and the angle of the ceiling, that she was in an attic.

Finally, as she felt her way across the space, she saw a sliver of light shining through the floor.

An attic door.

Her heart thudded harder.

She had to get out of here.

She pushed on the door in the floor. Just as she expected, nothing happened. As she felt alongside it, her fingers scraped something metal.

A backside of a lock. Somehow, someone had installed a locking mechanism on it.

*Think, Rachel. Think.*

How would Jonah tell her to get out of this situation?

Maybe she could pick the lock somehow. Even

though the keyhole was on the other side, maybe there was a way.

But with what?

She was wearing her pajamas, and she didn't exactly sleep with bobby pins in her hair. What could she use?

Maybe if she felt along the floor, she could find a piece of metal or a nail that was small enough to slide into the lock and release it.

It may not work, but at least it was something. The idea gave her a task to focus her thoughts on instead of the despair that wanted to creep in.

As she felt along the floor, she remembered that dream she'd been having.

She'd been on the verge of figuring out a solution for their problem, a drug to counteract the effects of the algae and jimsonweed.

She couldn't remember what it was anymore. Her dream had faded that quickly.

And so far, all she'd felt on the floor was sand, dirt, and dust bunnies.

She was about to search the middle of the floor when a footstep sounded nearby.

She froze, part of her not wanting to know what these men had planned for her.

The door opened, and a bright light hit her face.

She squinted against it as she stared at the silhouette of a man standing there below her.

The light behind the man was too bright for her to make out any of his features.

But as the guy said her name, she realized that his voice was familiar.

"WHAT DID YOU DO?" Jonah squeezed the phone so tightly he thought it might break as he stormed through the house.

"What are you talking about?" Larchmont sounded earnestly confused on the other end.

Jonah rushed into the front yard and ran to the end of the driveway, still desperate to find any signs of Rachel.

There were none.

"Did you come here to distract me while someone did something to Rachel?" Jonah paused, barely able to catch his breath. Not because he was out of shape, but because anger tried to consume him. The fiery emotion tightened his lungs and muscles until they ached. "And don't even think of lying to me."

"I have no idea what you're talking about." Larchmont's voice was even and mellow.

He sounded honest.

But Jonah wouldn't be that quick to trust him.

"While you and I were talking, somebody grabbed Rachel," Jonah said. "She's gone."

"What?" Larchmont paused as if earnestly surprised. "I promise you, I had nothing to do with that."

"So someone just happened to be watching and waiting for the moment I was distracted by you in the middle of the night to grab her?" Jonah hadn't been sure for a while that he could trust his boss. Those issues were coming into clarity now, it seemed.

"I don't know. I can't explain it because I had nothing to do with it. But Jonah . . . if Amar grabbed her . . ."

More anger—along with a touch of fear—burned inside Jonah. "I know."

"We've got to find her."

*We?* Jonah didn't ask that question out loud. This wasn't the time to get into it with his boss.

The only thing he needed to concentrate on now was finding Rachel.

Jonah gripped his phone harder. "I need to call Cassidy at the police station and let her know what's going on."

"You do that. I'll start looking into this also."

Larchmont's voice held dire warning. "Because if Amar and his men have Rachel, they'll want to use her base of knowledge and her skills for something sinister. I'm sure of it."

That was what Jonah feared too.

That and the idea that they might torture her until they got what they wanted.

Jonah had to find Rachel. There was no time to waste.

———

"Rex?" Rachel stared at the man in disbelief.

"I'm sorry it had to come down to this. But we had no other options." He stepped up into the room and tugged on a light, using a string Rachel hadn't seen in the dark.

His other hand rested in his pocket in a casual manner that made it seem like he did things such as abducting women every day.

Maybe he did. He could be a serial killer, for all Rachel knew.

"Why am I here?" She drew back, desperate to put space between her and this man. "Why are *you* here? Who are you really?"

"Not so many questions. Not yet." Then he paused. "On second thought, we don't have much time so maybe I should get right down to business.

You're a very valuable commodity."

Her hands fisted at her sides. "You showing up on this island wasn't an accident, was it? You had a plan all along."

"Most good businessmen do." He sounded smug as he said the words.

That fact only caused more determination to rise in her. "You're working for Amar."

His eyebrows flung up. "Amar?"

"Stop playing dumb. The two of you are planning an attack on the United States, and you're using Lantern Beach as a trial run."

A smile stretched across his lips as if he liked the way she'd worded that. Making him happy had *not* been her intention.

"You're not going to get away with this," she growled as disgust bubbled inside her.

He shrugged. "That's what they all say."

"I still don't know what you want from me."

His gaze locked on hers. "I need your brain."

"My brain?" She let out a little laugh. "I'm not going to help you hurt anyone!"

*That* was why they'd targeted her?

They could think again.

They were in for a rude awakening if they thought she would do their dirty work for them.

Rex only grunted with doubt. "We'll see about that."

Jonah . . . Jonah would find her. Would help her.

In an instant, she knew without a doubt that Jonah truly cared for her.

Was this how it all would end? Would they ever get their chance at happily-ever-after?

"So what do you want from me?" Her throat burned as she asked the question.

Part of her didn't want to know what his plan was. But she had no other choice but to hear him out —not when so much was on the line.

Rachel held her breath as she waited to hear what Rex had to say.

AS JONAH STOOD in the front yard of Rachel's place, Cassidy pulled into the driveway.

After he explained the situation again, she put out an APB for her officers to be on the lookout for Rachel.

But everything was closing in, and at any moment it felt like the pressure would reach the point of implosion.

Jonah couldn't believe he'd let Rachel be taken, especially when he'd been so close. But someone had been planning this. They'd been watching and waiting.

He fisted his hands at the thought of it.

One of her officers, Dane Bradshaw, brought his dog, Ranger. The canine was a boxer mix and a great police dog.

For the next hour, Bradshaw and Ranger tried to follow Rachel's scent. Jonah went with them.

But whoever had taken Rachel must have carried her onto the beach and then taken her to a car to get away. The scent stopped at the road about a quarter mile away from her house.

Bradshaw frowned. "Sometimes, canines can follow scents even in moving cars. But not today. The conditions aren't right. I'm sorry."

Jonah remained composed as he thanked him.

Then he headed back to Rachel's.

At the house, Jonah paused and leaned against the steps leading to the front door.

An overwhelming ache filled his chest until he thought his heart might physically stop.

A shadow appeared, and he looked up and saw Cassidy there.

"I can't let them hurt her, Cassidy." He croaked out the words.

"We're going to do everything in our power to protect Rachel." Cassidy leveled her gaze with his. "You have my word."

"These guys aren't dumb. They're not just going to enact this plan here on the island and then wait for you to capture them. You know there has to be more to this."

Cassidy frowned. "My thoughts exactly. There's something we haven't figured out yet. Maybe this is all just a distraction while they enact their plan elsewhere."

Jonah didn't like those implications, but Cassidy very well could be correct.

"Is the FBI keeping you in the loop, at least?" Jonah hoped the answer would be yes.

"I believe they are for the most part. But they haven't found very many answers either, unfortunately."

Jonah's mind raced.

Where would they have taken Rachel? Had they been able to get off the island?

Jonah didn't think that was a possibility.

But right now, this island was feeling awfully big.

———

"Now that William is dead, we need someone else to head up this project," Rex explained.

Rachel's lungs tightened. "Why did you kill him?"

"I'm not taking credit for that one, but I can say that he was no longer useful."

What did that mean? She didn't ask. She had too many other pressing questions.

"You're the one who sent that gunman after me, aren't you?" Rachel stared up at him, trying to put the pieces together. "And you sent someone to break into my house? You probably even sent that crazy man to my door and to my office window."

"I knew you were smart, and that's proving to be true," Rex said.

A tremble raked through Rachel.

These men were going to try to force her to do their dirty work.

When they were done, they would kill her.

She had to think of a way to get out of this situation.

But she knew she was trapped.

If Rachel refused to do what they said, she'd die . . . and if she cooperated, she'd also die.

# FORTY-THREE

AFTER A ROUND of searching the island, Jonah stood outside Rachel's house again.

He hadn't found any clues.

He was going to go back out.

But first, he wanted to check if there were new updates.

He headed toward Cassidy, who'd set up a temporary station in the front. But before he could ask any questions, a car pulled to a fast stop in the driveway.

Noelle rushed out, Gunner at her side.

"Gunner just told me what was happening." Noelle paused in front of Jonah, nearly sounding breathless. "Where's Rachel?"

His throat tightened. "Someone abducted her."

"What?" Noelle's hand flew over her mouth.

Gunner wrapped his arm around her and pulled her close.

"We've been searching the island and doing everything we know in order to find her," Jonah explained. "But we haven't been successful yet."

"Lantern Beach is locked down," Noelle said. "That should help, right?"

"In theory." Jonah didn't mention just how smart these men were. He was trying to keep the worry from his voice, so as not to upset Noelle.

But he knew that was useless. Noelle was a smart woman. She knew how serious this situation was.

Who was he kidding? Maybe he was trying to keep himself calm.

Noelle glanced at him, turbulence in her gaze. "Jonah . . . I have to wonder if maybe Rex Houghton is involved with this."

"Why Rex?"

She shrugged. "I don't know. It's just a feeling, I guess. Even when he stopped to talk to me on the boardwalk the other day, I got weird vibes from him. I tried to brush it off, but maybe I shouldn't have. I've been thinking about it ever since."

"I know how bad vibes work, but we're going to need something more than that," Jonah said.

She let out a breath. "One time, I Googled his company, just out of curiosity. Everything on his website was so vague. When I went on a couple of dates with him, he would never give me any direct answers. But then I started to think about the timing of his arrival here on the island . . ." She shrugged. "I don't know. Something has never felt right about him."

"What do you mean?"

"I just mean . . . I think there's more to him."

Jonah nodded. "Maybe I should go talk to him."

Gunner stepped forward. "Would you like me to go with you?"

Jonah nodded at Noelle. "I would. But I think you're better off staying with Noelle . . . especially until we know what's going on."

Gunner didn't argue.

With that thought, Jonah started toward his SUV.

———

Only one car was parked outside Rex's place, and all the lights were out.

But that didn't stop Jonah.

He rushed toward the door and pressed the doorbell, his finger lingering on the button to extend the sound. He didn't even wait two seconds before he began pounding on the door as well.

He needed to know if Rex knew anything. It appeared the man was home.

If this guy had answers, Jonah wanted them.

After ringing the bell and knocking for probably five minutes, the door finally opened.

A sleepy-looking Rex Houghton stood there. He wore plaid pajama bottoms and a white T-shirt that made him appear as if he had just awoken. Plus, his hair was tussled and messy looking.

"Can I help you?" Rex rubbed a hand over his face.

"Where's Rachel?" Jonah demanded.

"Who?" A knot formed on his brow.

The liar.

"Rachel Atwood," Jonah repeated, his irritation growing. "Don't tell me you don't know where she is."

"I'm not even sure I know who she is, nonetheless where she is."

"Stop playing dumb. You met her earlier this week on the boardwalk when she and Noelle were having breakfast together. I saw it with my own eyes."

"Oh . . ." Realization washed over his features. "*That* was her name. Okay, so yes, I have met her. But why in the world would I know where she is?"

"Because I know you came to this island with ulterior motives. So why don't you just fess up to your involvement in this whole fiasco? There's no need to draw this out."

"You mean the water issue?" A dry chuckle

captured his voice. "Why would I have anything to do with that?"

"You tell me." Jonah narrowed his eyes. "If you're innocent in this, then you won't mind me looking inside your house."

Rex stared at Jonah a moment before stepping back. "Of course. Be my guest."

Jonah withdrew his gun and braced himself for what he might find.

RACHEL HAD HEARD the sound downstairs.

A doorbell.

Was someone here?

Should she scream?

As soon as the bell chimed, Rex motioned to someone standing near the door.

A guard stepped into the attic.

"Take care of her," Rex muttered. "Make sure she's quiet. If she's not, I'll kill whoever is at the door."

The man took Rachel by the bicep, squeezing so hard that she nearly yelped. But she refused to give him that satisfaction.

He led her through the attic to another room.

A room that had been set up like a . . . lab.

The space wasn't large—probably six by six—with a workstation along one wall. Numerous pieces of equipment and supplies were on a shelf there. The room had been lined with some kind of white plastic insulation that made it stunningly bright and sterile.

"What do you expect me to do?" Her voice trembled as she stared at the state-of-the-art equipment he had there.

"You need to come up with the remedy to the toxic bacteria we created," the man barked. "That way, if anyone important gets sick, we know they'll ultimately be okay."

"Why me? This isn't my specialty."

"We know all about your PhDs. Your areas of study. Your skill level. We feel confident you can accomplish this."

Rachel's throat tightened.

How was she going to get out of this situation?

She had no idea.

But she would need to think quickly.

"This won't be a fast process," she told him.

"You're going to have to speed things up a bit." The man glared at her. "Now, there's no more time to talk. Get busy. Soon, this whole island is going to be sick. Going crazy. It's just a taste of our larger plan."

She shook her head, horrified at the ease with which this man talked about harming others. "Why would you want people to suffer like this?"

He smirked. "Because you're all enemies."

———

Jonah should have brought someone with him. But it was too late for that. At least he had his gun.

He stepped into Rex's house, his eyes wide open and his body on alert.

Could Rachel be here?

If not, then where would she be?

He didn't have any other ideas. But this place was his best chance. However, the ease at which Rex let him inside raised all kind of suspicions.

Jonah glanced behind him and saw Rex standing at the door, that smirk still on his face.

He was watching everything Jonah did.

Had he expected Jonah to come here? Had he set up some kind of trap?

Jonah couldn't be sure. But he needed to remain on guard.

He checked the first level, but there was no sign of Rachel. Then he went to the second floor and searched the bedrooms.

Rex followed and stood near the top of the steps, still watching.

Not only were there no signs of Rachel, but there were no signs of anything nefarious either.

Yet Jonah sensed this guy was somehow involved.

But how would he prove it?

That was what he needed to figure out.

He had no time to waste.

# CHAPTER
# FORTY-FIVE

THE GUARD REMAINED STATIONED at the door.

He didn't say anything else. He only watched her while holding his gun.

Where exactly was she on the island?

In a house, she could only assume.

If she yelled or cried out, would someone hear her? Or would Rex really kill the person at the door?

She wouldn't put it past him.

She glanced around. The ceiling had insulation—thick and rubbery and new.

She would guess they had soundproofed the place pretty well.

These guys were too smart not to have thought through some of these details.

But she knew for certain that Jonah would look for her.

When he did, she needed to be able to alert him.

She glanced over her shoulder at the guard as he watched her.

"What?" the man snapped.

She shrugged. "I'm just trying to put the pieces together."

"The only pieces you need to put together are this antibiotic that will cure this infection."

Her muscles tensed even more as she turned back to her workstation.

She'd meant it when she told the guard these things took time.

But everyone around her seemed unconvinced of that.

*Think, Rachel. There's got to be something you can do.*

She glanced around.

Her eyes stopped on a couple of chemicals they'd provided for her.

Wait . . . she could . . .

She nibbled on her bottom lip.

Would that really work?

It might be the only choice she had.

But her plan could backfire.

Sweat sprinkled across her skin.

She had to do it.

But she had to wait until the timing was just right.

Rex looked at Jonah with that same smug expression as Jonah headed back downstairs in defeat. He hadn't found anything. But that didn't mean there wasn't some kind of secret space within the house. He'd searched for any hidden doors in the walls or ceiling but hadn't seen anything.

"See?" Rex said. "You feel better now?"

"Not really." Jonah locked gazes with Rex as he paused by the front door. "I know you have something to do with this."

Rex shrugged. "I'm sorry you think that. But you're wasting your time here."

Jonah knew that wasn't true.

But he would need to get someone else involved right now if he wanted to find answers.

Someone like Cassidy—someone who had power to get things done.

Jonah could hear the clock ticking in his head and knew he didn't have any time to waste.

Yet he felt certain Rex knew something that he wasn't letting on.

What had Jonah missed inside? He'd looked in the closets. Paid attention for any signs of hidden rooms. There had been nothing.

He glared at Rex again before taking a step toward his car.

He was going to need to talk to Cassidy.

Jonah paused beside his Jeep and stared up at that beach house again.

What secret was it holding? Could Rachel be in there somewhere?

He pressed his eyes closed. *God, give me answers. Please. Not only for Rachel's sake but for this entire country's . . .*

—————

Rachel sensed her time running out.

If she was going to act, it needed to be soon.

She glanced at those chemicals again.

The armed guard was still behind her, but the door was open.

He had keys on his belt and a gun in his hands.

She sucked in a breath, praying for courage.

If things went badly, she could die.

But at least she wouldn't have had any part in all of this.

That seemed like reason enough to risk it all.

Before she could second-guess herself, she casually reached over and grabbed some peroxide. Acting as if she was doing testing, she poured some in a beaker. She felt confident this guy wouldn't have a clue what she was really doing.

He was just the muscle behind this operation.

She held her breath before she enacted the next part of her plan.

Carefully, she grabbed some potassium.

She glanced at the guard.

Saw he stood beside the entrance.

Just where she needed him.

She quickly mixed the chemicals together.

Instantly, fire ignited.

She flung the beaker at the guard.

As it hit his shoulder, his shirt erupted into flames, and he screamed with pain. He dropped to the floor and rolled around.

"Sorry," she murmured.

Before he could reach her, Rachel grabbed the keys from his belt.

As he writhed on the floor, trying to put the fire out, flames caught the walls. They began to burn.

She had to get out of here.

Now.

Wasting no more time, she grabbed the man's gun and headed toward the exit.

She shoved the ladder down.

She still had Rex to deal with.

But she could already smell the smoke in the air.

Before the ladder even hit the bottom, she scrambled down the steps. At the bottom, she realized she was in some kind of closet. Somehow, Rex had walled up this space.

Quickly, she pressed the paneling in front of her.

It opened.

Relief filled her.

She sprang into motion again and darted down the hallway.

As she reached the first floor, a dark figure appeared in front of her.

Rex.

Just as she'd expected.

"What do you think you're doing?" he muttered.

Rachel raised her gun. "This."

JUST BEFORE JONAH pulled out of the driveway to head away from Rex's place, he paused.

Was that smoke coming from the roof?

He stared at the house a moment longer.

It was.

And it wasn't coming from a chimney. No one had a fire this time of year. It was too hot outside.

At once, Jonah remembered Rex's messy hair.

It was more than messy. Had there been dust in it?

He threw on his brakes and parked.

As he did, flames shot through the roof.

Acting quickly, he called Cassidy and told her what was going on.

Then he jumped out of the SUV and ran toward the house.

That fire wasn't a coincidence.

What if Rachel *was* inside but hidden?

He didn't know, but he was going to find out.

He raced back toward the front door, gun drawn.

He didn't bother to knock this time.

Using his shoulder, he threw the door open and raised his Sig.

As soon as he did, he saw Rachel standing at the top of the stairs.

She held a gun in her trembling hands.

Rex had his own gun raised.

It was a three-way standoff.

The truth was none of them had much time right now. Not with the house going up in flames.

As if on cue, sirens sounded in the distance.

First responders had already been deployed.

"You aren't going to mess up our plan," Rex said with a sneer. "It's already too late. Everything has already been set in motion."

"If you mean the fact that you're targeting other water treatment plants, we already have people acting on that," Jonah told him.

Doubt flickered in Rex's gaze.

"Everything is set in motion," Rex insisted.

For a moment, Jonah wondered if there was more than what met the eye.

But maybe Rex was just bluffing.

If Jonah was going to act, he needed to act quickly.

But one wrong move could end with a bullet coming at Rachel.

Just then, the flames licked closer, coming down the walls on the second story.

At any moment, this house would be engulfed in fire.

Jonah glanced up again.

Saw that part of the ceiling on the second floor was starting to collapse.

"Look out!" Jonah shouted.

Rex looked up.

Rachel ducked.

Jonah pulled the trigger.

Rex fell to the floor.

As he did, Jonah ran up the stairs and grabbed Rachel's hand.

"Come on. We need to get out of here."

But before they could reach the door, a beam fell, blocking them from escaping.

———

Rachel bit back her scream when she saw the fiery beam in front of them.

Jonah paused and turned, heading toward the other side of the house to another exit.

Before they could move, a voice cut through the roar of the fire. "You're not going to walk out of this alive."

She swerved her head toward the voice.

Rex.

Despite the gunshot wound to his chest, he had his gun raised.

Before he could pull the trigger, Jonah pushed her down and covered her body with his.

The bullet missed her.

Her heart pounded out of control.

But what if it had hit Jonah?

She glanced at him.

He seemed okay.

The next moment, he sprang to life. Drew his gun. Pulled the trigger again.

The bullet hit Rex's hand this time, and he let out a moan.

Quickly, Jonah scrambled to his feet. Pulled Rachel up after him.

They ran toward the back stairway.

Just as they stepped outside onto the deck and scrambled down the steps, another crash sounded behind them.

The house had become consumed quickly.

But they were out.

They were safe.

For now.

Rachel wasn't sure that this nightmare was over.

Not yet at least.

Because there was something they were still missing.

Someone else who was involved.

She was sure of it.

Rex wasn't Draco.

Then who was?

# CHAPTER
# FORTY-SEVEN

JONAH SLIPPED his arm around Rachel as they watched firefighters extinguish the flames. Smoke still hung in the air, mingling with the salty scent of the ocean. Darkness surrounded them as the night stretched on.

Rex had survived. They'd managed to get him out before the place was consumed.

The guard upstairs had also made it to a window and jumped out. He was badly injured and was being treated at the hospital.

Jonah supposed that was a good thing—at least for Rachel's sake. Living with yourself after taking another's life was a burden he didn't want her to carry.

"I'm so glad you're okay," he murmured into her ear.

She leaned close to him, nestling in the crook of his arm. "Me too."

"Maybe this is all over."

"I wish I could say that. But I don't think it is."

"What do you mean?"

"I mean . . . something Rex said to me. He indicated that he wasn't the one who'd killed William. I think someone else is involved."

"We need to tell Cassidy." Amar? Larchmont? Those seemed like the most obvious choices.

Rachel nodded. "I know."

Just then, Cassidy walked toward them. "What a night."

"Cassidy," Rachel started.

But before she could explain anything, another vehicle pulled onto the scene. Dr. Hensley rushed out and hurried toward them. "I just heard what happened. Are you okay?"

"I'm fine," Rachel said.

Jonah pulled her closer, thankful she was still with him. That could have turned out a lot differently.

"What happened?" Dr. Hensley continued.

Rachel stiffened then froze.

Pulling out of Jonah's arms, she turned to her boss. Her entire demeanor changed from frightened and exhausted into someone with purpose.

"I think you know," Rachel muttered.

Jonah stiffened. What did she mean by that?

He was about to find out.

————

"You're the other one involved in this, aren't you?" Rachel stared at her boss.

Hensley jerked his head back as if in shock. "What?"

"You're somehow involved in this. You got William into the middle of it also." Her thoughts continued to race.

He let out a laugh. "Rachel . . . are you sure you're okay right now?"

"I'm more than sure I'm okay. It was you." She hadn't realized it until now.

But suddenly, the name Draco made sense.

"Maybe a paramedic should look at her." Hensley glanced around as if looking for one.

Cassidy stepped forward. "Let her speak."

Rachel rose up to full height, determined not to back down. "I don't think William is the type to be the mastermind behind this. He wouldn't have had the connections to sell this to a terrorist organization."

"She has a point," Jonah said.

"You told us a story once at a meeting about a time in college you dressed up like Dracula," Rachel reminded him. "Afterward, everyone started calling you Draco—because you also happened to be working on a project involving the use of blood in beauty treatments."

"I think you're mistaken," Hensley muttered.

"You only mentioned it once, and it was only briefly," Rachel continued. "I couldn't remember why the name seemed familiar. But that's why. You used that name when you worked with that research facility in Arizona." Rachel gasped as another more potent realization hit her. "It's your wife."

"Leave my wife out of this." Hensley's gaze darkened.

"No, she wasn't involved with the nefarious part of this plan," Rachel continued. "But she loves looking young. Her cosmetic surgeries probably cost you an arm and a leg. In fact, maybe they put you deeply in debt."

Hensley didn't say anything.

"You asked William to look into a solution for you. I mean, he's brilliant, and facial serums were his specialty. But you wanted him to discover something that broke through the mold of Ocean Essence's promise of staying all natural. You asked him to develop something synthetic."

"You don't know what you're talking about."

Rachel didn't let his words stop her. "What William accidentally created was something with harmful effects on some people. You knew it wouldn't work for your wife. But then another idea formed in your mind. What if you could sell it? There had to be someone who would be interested in something with such psychedelic effects. My guess is that you somehow had a connection with Rex, and that connection is what led him to move to this island."

"I always thought his move here seemed suspicious." Cassidy stared at Hensley.

Rachel glanced at him. She noticed how sweat began to form across his brow.

They were hitting the nail on the head, weren't they?

"You don't know anything," he finally snapped.

"You know how the clinical trial process works," Rachel continued, pretending like she didn't hear him. "You set up that facility in Arizona. But Rex and his people pressured you. He knew there was no way everyone would use a facial lotion. They needed something more universal. That's when they demanded you figure out a way to infiltrate the water system with this new toxic combination you developed."

Hensley didn't deny her words, so she continued.

"You would need to bring in truckloads of a toxin to infect an entire water system, and that would be nearly impossible to do unnoticed. That's when you realized you could use a bacterium like bacillus stearothermophilus. It doubles in size every ten minutes. If you could infuse the algae and the jimsonweed with this bacterium, you'd have just the solution you needed."

"Stop!" His face reddened. "I didn't want anything to do with that. I wanted out."

So he was admitting his involvement?

Good.

"What happened?" Cassidy crossed her arms as she waited for his response.

"Look, I'll tell you. But I want some kind of immunity." Desperation singed his every word.

"I can't promise you that," Cassidy said. "What you did could have harmed thousands of people—if not more."

Sweat now covered every inch of visible skin. "I told them no! But they wouldn't listen."

"You're the one who killed William, aren't you?" Rachel's voice trailed with surprise at the revelation. "You set everything up so William and I would take the fall. That's why my name was on the project out in Arizona. But you could see William was getting antsy, and you got scared. Then Rex's guys showed up on the island, and you knew something was going down. That's why your wife is nowhere around, isn't it?"

He seemed to pull himself together and raised his chin. "I don't have anything more to say."

"You've said plenty." Cassidy pulled out her handcuffs. "You're under arrest for involvement in acts of terrorism and murder, among other things."

"What about Amar?" Jonah asked.

"Am-who?" Hensley stared at him in confusion.

Wait . . . Amar wasn't involved in this?

Rachel glanced at Jonah.

Then what exactly did that mean?

TWO DAYS LATER, the chaos on Lantern Beach seemed to calm down.

And Jonah couldn't be happier.

The island's water was cleared and deemed safe.

Doctors had figured out the correct antibiotic to treat people. Now, many who were on the island were in recovery and expected to be okay.

The woman who'd called Rachel, Sharon Wilson, had been rescued. The trials hadn't yet started on her yet, so she was still in her right mind.

Sharon had told police she stole a phone from one of the employees and escaped. Before that, she'd overheard a conversation between some of the people running the trials. One of the men had mentioned that Rachel Atwood was their best hope of finding a cure for the effects of the lotion.

Sharon's daughter had also done the trial with her, and the effects of the lotion on her were harsh—and scary. Because of that, Sharon had taken off through the desert to find help. She'd walked, trying to find cell service.

She'd tried to call the police, but she hadn't had a strong enough connection. Turns out, she found Rachel's number stored in the phone. She decided to try to call Rachel also.

When there had been no cell service, she'd kept walking.

Eventually, she tried the police again. While she was waiting for them to pick her up, she'd tried Rachel again.

But by the time anyone found her, she was passed out, dehydrated, and her phone was dead.

Thankfully, she was now recovering in an Arizona hospital.

Six bodies total had been found in Arizona.

Rex was an arms dealer who'd promised several terrorist groups that he had just the biological agent they needed. They'd all wanted proof first.

That was when he'd decided to target Lantern Beach.

Rex had been arrested in addition to Dr. Hensley and several men Rex and Hensley had hired. Most worked for an organization called Dagger, the arch nemesis of Blackout. The group was known for their notorious involvement in illegal operations.

It turned out Hensley was in debt for more than one million thanks to his wife's surgeries and shopping sprees. He was desperate for a way out—no matter the cost.

Even better, Amar Ravish had been arrested by the FBI.

Yes, arrested.

They'd encountered him during the island's lockdown, recognized him, and he'd been taken into custody.

Amar had come here to try to make Jonah pay for shooting his brother. Thankfully, he hadn't been successful.

Jonah wanted to put that all in the past.

He rang the bell at Rachel's place and waited.

They were going on a date tonight.

Roman answered. He'd arrived back yesterday. From what Jonah had heard, his meeting had gone well. His investor was interested in the product, and they'd made a tentative deal.

At least that should put Roman in a good mood. Maybe that would work in Jonah's favor.

The man nodded at Jonah. "Did you figure out a way to get back in my daughter's good graces?"

"I'm trying really hard."

"Good. As you should be. I don't like seeing my daughter upset."

"I assure you, neither do I, sir."

Roman locked gazes with Jonah. "One more chance, and if you blow it this time, you're out for good. Understand?"

Jonah nodded. "Absolutely."

"Dad . . ." Rachel appeared behind her father and looped her arm through her dad's.

Jonah sucked in a breath at the sight of her.

She looked so beautiful in the sundress with her hair falling below her shoulders. The slightly discolored patches from vitiligo on her shoulders did nothing to mar her beauty. In fact, they just made her look more unique.

"You're not giving him a hard time, are you?" Rachel asked her dad.

Roman shrugged. "I'm doing my duty."

She patted his arm. "I'm a big girl."

"You'll always be my baby."

She nearly glowed at him. "I know. And I love you for that."

She kissed her father's cheek.

Then she turned to Jonah. "You ready?"

He sucked in a deep breath. "I am."

Now he only hoped he didn't blow this.

———

Rachel felt surprisingly nervous as she stepped outside with Jonah.

It wasn't as if they hadn't done this uncountable times before. But somehow, this time felt different.

She'd even worn her favorite floral dress, a sweater, and sandals.

Jonah looked handsome in his khakis, a button-up shirt, and a jean jacket. There was a slight breeze on the island tonight, which should make for the perfect evening.

He helped her into his vehicle, and they took off.

Rachel wasn't even sure where they were going.

Another fact that made her a little nervous.

So much had happened over the past several days.

Rachel's conclusions had been mostly correct.

Hensley had hired someone to kill William, and he was trying to frame Rachel for everything. Meanwhile, he had planned to announce his retirement and get out of the country. The FBI found the plane tickets for Hensley and his wife, and even a letter of resignation. He planned on claiming the stress of everything was too much for him and his health.

He had tried to stop the whole thing from growing as big as it had. But he'd been unsuccessful, and that was when he realized he wanted out.

But he was already in too deep.

Jonah pulled to a stop at a beach parking area.

Her eyebrows shot up.

This hadn't been what she was expecting.

He opened her door for her before reaching into the back of his Jeep. He grabbed a picnic basket.

"Impressive," Rachel muttered.

"Don't be too impressed. I had Lisa put this together for me."

Rachel smiled. "That's still impressive."

He led her down a path to the beach to where the sun was beginning to set. As she saw the rolling ocean waves just over the dune, she paused.

"I love this island," she murmured. "It's been through a lot over the past several months."

"You can say that again." Jonah paused beside her and stared ahead also.

These peaceful, secluded shores seemed to be the perfect location for evil men to enact their plans. It had been that way for a long time—since pirates had discovered this beautiful place more than three hundred years ago.

"But good has come out of everything, hasn't it?" Rachel continued. "I mean, Noelle found Gunner, the new theater that opened here is thriving, we've had a wedding, and bad guys have been put behind bars."

"And I found you." Jonah gave her a lingering glance.

Her cheeks warmed, and she reached over to

squeeze his hand. "One of the biggest blessings of all."

He leaned toward her and kissed her cheek.

Then, hand in hand, they continued over the dune.

A picnic area had already been set up there, including a small coffee table covered in a seafoam-colored cloth, some oversized pillows to sit on, and even a centerpiece—a Scrabble board.

She paused and looked at him. "You did this?"

"I had some help." He shrugged. "There have been so many secretive things happening on these shores. I thought one of those should be a good memory."

She grinned. "I love it."

He took her hand and led her to one of the pillows. As she sat and began sipping a drink he poured for her, he set up their dinner. Grilled chicken, pasta salad, bread, and cheesecake for dessert.

Rachel could hardly think about her food or even the game, however.

"I can't wait anymore," she said as she turned to him. "I'm not going to be able to eat a bite until I know what you're thinking."

"Understood." He turned toward her, the sunset casting pink shadows across his face. "Rachel, I messed up when I left you here in Lantern Beach. I was trying to protect you, but I should have simply talked to you about it so we could decide our future together."

"Yes, you should have."

A grin flickered across his face. "You're the most wonderful woman I've ever met. I feel safe when I'm with you. I feel loved. Like I belong. And that's not something I've often felt."

Rachel reached forward and skimmed her fingers across his jaw. She knew all about how difficult it had been for him to grow up in the foster care system.

"I don't deserve a second chance, but I'm here to beg you for one." His gaze locked with hers. "What do you think?"

"I think we have some things to figure out."

"I agree." He swallowed hard. "I've been offered a job with Blackout, and I'd like to take it."

Her eyes lit. "Really? I've always thought you'd be a good fit for them."

"I think so too."

"What did Larchmont think?"

"He's not too happy, but he has a new group of recruits to work for him. I think he'll be okay."

"More guys like you?"

Jonah nodded.

"How many of you are there?"

"Too many." He shrugged. "What about your career with Ocean Essence?"

"I'm not sure. At first, I was certain they would shut down the facilities here. But I just got word a couple of hours ago that they'd like to keep this lab open."

"Really? That's surprising."

Rachel nodded. "For me too. They'd like this facility to concentrate on the line I'm overseeing—the dermatological side of things."

"Who would lead it?"

A smile tugged at her lips. "Me."

"What?" His eyes lit. "That's great news."

She pulled her legs beneath her and lifted her face to the wind. "I'm trying to figure out if I want to accept."

"Why wouldn't you?"

Rachel shrugged. "There's just a lot going on."

"I understand. What are you thinking?"

She leaned closer, feeling the sparkle in her gaze. "I'm thinking if you stay here then it's a no-brainer."

Jonah grinned. "I was hoping you might say that."

Rachel's smile dimmed for a moment. "I don't want you giving up everything for me."

"You'd be worth it. But I really am ready for this change."

"You mean it?"

He scooted closer. "More than anything. I've always wondered about my name. Jonah. The man who ran from God and ended up being swallowed by a big fish. I always thought a big fish would have to swallow me for me to make any changes. I just didn't realize how I was running from my calling. It took you almost dying for me to realize that you're the future I've always wanted."

Rachel didn't have to think about her response for long. "Then I'd love nothing more than for you and me to give us another chance."

The next instant, his grin widened, and his lips met hers.

Rachel knew in her gut that this was the start of many more kisses.

And she couldn't be happier about it.

~~~

Thank you for reading *Secret Shores*. If you enjoyed this book, please consider leaving a review!
~~~

# ALSO BY CHRISTY BARRITT:

# YOU ALSO MIGHT ENJOY THESE OTHER BOOKS IN THE LANTERN BEACH SERIES:

## LANTERN BEACH MYSTERIES

### Hidden Currents

*You can take the detective out of the investigation, but you can't take the investigator out of the detective.* A notorious gang puts a bounty on Detective Lady Matthews's head after she takes down their leader, leaving her no choice but to hide until she can testify at trial. But her temporary home across the country on a remote North Carolina island isn't as peaceful as she initially thinks. Living under the new identity of Cassidy Livingston, she struggles to keep her investigative skills tucked away, especially after a body washes ashore. When local police bungle the murder investigation, she can't resist stepping in. But Cassidy is supposed to be keeping a low profile. One wrong move could lead to both her discovery and her demise. Can she bring justice to the island . . . or will the hidden currents surrounding her pull her under for good?

**Flood Watch**

*The tide is high, and so is the danger on Lantern Beach.* Still in hiding after infiltrating a dangerous gang, Cassidy Livingston just has to make it a few more months before she can testify at trial and resume her old life. But trouble keeps finding her, and Cassidy is pulled into a local investigation after a man mysteriously disappears from the island she now calls home. A recurring nightmare from her time undercover only muddies things, as does a visit from the parents of her handsome ex-Navy SEAL neighbor. When a friend's life is threatened, Cassidy must make choices that put her on the verge of blowing her cover. With a flood watch on her emotions and her life in a tangle, will Cassidy find the truth? Or will her past finally drown her?

**Storm Surge**

*A storm is brewing hundreds of miles away, but its effects are devastating even from afar.* Laid-back, loose, and light: that's Cassidy Livingston's new motto. But when a makeshift boat with a bloody cloth inside washes ashore near her oceanfront home, her detective instincts shift into gear . . . again. Seeking clues isn't the only thing on her mind—romance is heating up with next-door neighbor and former Navy SEAL Ty Chambers as well. Her heart wants the love and stability she's longed for her entire life. But her hidden identity only leads to a tidal wave of turbulence. As more answers emerge about the boat, the danger around her rises, creating a treacherous swell that threatens to reveal her past. Can Cassidy mind her own business, or will the storm surge of violence and corruption that has washed ashore on Lantern Beach leave her life in wreckage?

## Dangerous Waters

*Danger lurks on the horizon, leaving only two choices: find shelter or flee.* Cassidy Livingston's new identity has begun to feel as comfortable as her favorite sweater. She's been tucked away on Lantern Beach for weeks, waiting to testify against a deadly gang, and is settling in to a new life she wants to last forever. When she thinks she spots someone malevolent from her past, panic swells inside her. If an enemy has found her, Cassidy won't be the only one who's a target. Everyone she's come to love will also be at risk. Dangerous waters threaten to pull her into an overpowering chasm she may never escape. Can Cassidy survive what lies ahead? Or has the tide fatally turned against her?

**Perilous Riptide**

Just when the current seems safer, an unseen danger emerges and threatens to destroy everything. When Cassidy Livingston finds a journal hidden deep in the recesses of her ice cream truck, her curiosity kicks into high gear. Islanders suspect that Elsa, the journal's owner, didn't die accidentally. Her final entry indicates their suspicions might be correct and that what Elsa observed on her final night may have led to her demise. Against the advice of Ty Chambers, her former Navy SEAL boyfriend, Cassidy taps into her detective skills and hunts for answers. But her search only leads to a skeletal body and trouble for both of them. As helplessness threatens to drown her, Cassidy is desperate to turn back time. Can Cassidy find what she needs to navigate the perilous situation? Or will the riptide surrounding her threaten everyone and everything Cassidy loves?

**Deadly Undertow**

The current's fatal pull is powerful, but so is one detective's will to live. When someone from Cassidy Livingston's past shows up on Lantern Beach and warns her of impending peril, opposing currents collide, threatening to drag her under. Running would be easy. But leaving would break her heart. Cassidy must decipher between the truth and lies, between reality and deception. Even more importantly, she must decide whom to trust and whom to fear. Her life depends on it. As danger rises and answers surface, everything Cassidy thought she knew is tested. In order to survive, Cassidy must take drastic measures and end the battle against the ruthless gang DH-7 once and for all. But if her final mission fails, the consequences will be as deadly as the raging undertow.

## LANTERN BEACH ROMANTIC SUSPENSE

### Tides of Deception

Change has come to Lantern Beach: a new police chief, a new season, and . . . a new romance? Austin Brooks has loved Skye Lavinia from the moment they met, but the walls she keeps around her seem impenetrable. Skye knows Austin is the best thing to ever happen to her. Yet she also knows that if he learns the truth about her past, he'd be a fool not to run. A chance encounter brings secrets bubbling to the surface, and danger soon follows. Are the life-threatening events plaguing them really accidents . . . or is someone trying to send a deadly message? With the tides on Lantern Beach come deception and lies. One question remains—who will be swept away as the water shifts? And will it bring the end for Austin and Skye, or merely the beginning?

**Shadow of Intrigue**

For her entire life, Lisa Garth has felt like a supporting character in the drama of life. The designation never bothered her—until now. Lantern Beach, where she's settled and runs a popular restaurant, has boarded up for the season. The slower pace leaves her with too much time alone. Braden Dillinger came to Lantern Beach to try to heal. The former Special Forces officer returned from battle with invisible scars and diminished hope. But his recovery is hampered by the fact that an unknown enemy is trying to kill him. From the moment Lisa and Braden meet, danger ignites around them, and both are drawn into a web of intrigue that turns their lives upside down. As shadows creep in, will Lisa and Braden be able to shine a light on the peril around them? Or will the encroaching darkness turn their worst nightmares into reality?

**Storm of Doubt**

A pastor who's lost faith in God. A romance writer who's lost faith in love. A faceless man with a deadly obsession. Nothing has felt right in Pastor Jack Wilson's world since his wife died two years ago. He hoped coming to Lantern Beach might help soothe the ragged edges of his soul. Instead, he feels more alone than ever. Novelist Juliette Grace came to the island to hide away. Though her professional life has never been better, her personal life has imploded. Her husband left her and a stalker's threats have grown more and more dangerous. When Jack saves Juliette from an attack, he sees the terror in her gaze and knows he must protect her. But when danger strikes again, will Jack be able to keep her safe? Or will the approaching storm prove too strong to withstand?

**Winds of Danger**

Wes O'Neill is perfectly content to hang with his friends and enjoy island life on Lantern Beach. Something begins to change inside him when Paige Henderson sweeps into his life. But the beautiful newcomer is hiding painful secrets beneath her cheerful facade. Police dispatcher Paige Henderson came to Lantern Beach riddled with guilt and uncertainties after the fallout of a bad relationship. When she meets Wes, she begins to open up to the possibility of love again. But there's something Wes isn't telling her—something that could change everything. As the winds shift, doubts seep into Paige's mind. Can Paige and Wes trust each other, even as the currents work against them? Or is trouble from the past too much to overcome?

**Rains of Remorse**

A stranger invades her home, leaving Rebecca

Jarvis terrified. Above all, she must protect the baby growing inside her. Since her estranged husband died suspiciously six months earlier, Rebecca has been determined to depend on no one but herself. Her chivalrous new neighbor appears to be an answer to prayer. But who is Levi Stoneman really? Rebecca wants to believe he can help her, but she can't ignore her instincts. As danger closes in, both Rebecca and Levi must figure out whom they can trust. With Rebecca's baby coming soon, there's no time to waste. Can the truth prevail . . . or will remorse overpower the best of intentions?

**Torrents of Fear**

The woman lingering in the crowd can't be Allison . . . can she? Because Allison was pronounced dead six years ago. Musician Carter Denver knows only one person who's capable of helping him find answers: Sadie Thompson, his estranged best friend and someone who also knew Allison. He needs to know if he's losing his mind or if Allison could have survived her car accident. Could Allison really be alive? If so, why is she trying to harm Carter and Sadie? As the two try to find answers, can Sadie keep her feelings for Carter hidden? Could he ever care for her, or is the man of her dreams still in love with the woman now causing his nightmares?

<h1 style="text-align:center">LANTERN BEACH PD</h1>

**On the Lookout**

*A runaway woman. A dead body. A mysterious compound.* When Cassidy Chambers accepted the job as police chief on Lantern Beach, she knew the island had its secrets. But a suspicious death with potentially far-reaching implications will test all her skills —and threaten to reveal her true identity. Cassidy enlists the help of her husband, former Navy SEAL Ty Chambers. As they dig for answers, both uncover parts of their pasts that are best left buried. Not everything is as it seems, and they must figure out if their John Doe is connected to the secretive group that has moved onto the island. As facts materialize, danger on the island grows. Can Cassidy and Ty discover the truth about the shadowy crimes in their cozy community? Or has darkness permanently invaded their beloved Lantern Beach?

**Attempt to Locate**

A fun girls' night out turns into a nightmare when armed robbers barge into the store where Cassidy and her friends are shopping. As the situation escalates and the men escape, a massive manhunt launches on Lantern Beach to apprehend the dangerous trio. In the midst of the chaos, a potential foe asks for Cassidy's help. He needs to find his sister who fled from the secretive Gilead's Cove community on the island. But the more Cassidy learns about the seemingly untouchable group, the more her unease grows. The pressure to solve both cases continues to mount. But as the gravity of the situation rises, so does the danger. Cassidy is determined to protect the island and break up the cult . . . but doing so might cost her everything.

**First Degree Murder**

Police Chief Cassidy Chambers longs for a break from the recent crimes plaguing Lantern Beach. She simply wants to enjoy her friends' upcoming wedding, to prepare for the busy tourist season about to slam the island, and to gather all the dirt she can on the suspicious community that's invaded the town. But trouble explodes on the island, sending residents—including Cassidy—into a squall of uneasiness. Cassidy may have more than one enemy plotting her demise, and the collateral damage seems unthinkable. As the temperature rises, so does the pressure to find answers. Someone is determined that Lantern Beach would be better off without their new police chief. And for Cassidy, one wrong move could mean certain death.

**Dead on Arrival**

With a highly charged local election consuming

the community, Police Chief Cassidy Chambers braces herself for a challenging day of breaking up petty conflicts and tamping down high emotions. But when widespread food poisoning spreads among potential voters across the island, Cassidy smells something rotten in the air. As Cassidy examines every possibility to uncover what's going on, local enigma Anthony Gilead again comes on her radar. The man is running for mayor and his cult-like following is growing at an alarming rate. Cassidy feels certain he has a spy embedded in her inner circle. The problem is that her pool of suspects gets deeper every day. Can Cassidy get to the bottom of what's eating away at her peaceful island home? Will voters turn out despite the outbreak of illness plaguing their tranquil town? And the even bigger question: Has darkness come to stay on Lantern Beach?

**Plan of Action**

*A missing Navy SEAL. Danger at the boiling point. The ultimate showdown.* When Police Chief Cassidy Chambers' husband, Ty, disappears, her world is turned upside down. His truck is discovered with blood inside, crashed in a ditch on Lantern Beach, but he's nowhere to be found. As they launch a manhunt to find him, Cassidy discovers that someone on the island has a deadly obsession with

Ty. Meanwhile, Gilead's Cove seems to be imploding. As danger heightens, federal law enforcement officials are called in. The cult's growing threat could lead to the pinnacle standoff of good versus evil. A clear plan of action is needed or the results will be devastating. Will Cassidy find Ty in time, or will she face a gut-wrenching loss? Will Anthony Gilead finally be unmasked for who he really is and be brought to justice? Hundreds of innocent lives are at stake . . . and not everyone will come out alive.

## LANTERN BEACH ESCAPE

**Afterglow**

*What if you married someone, only to discover that she was suspected of killing her former fiancé?* While on their honeymoon, Grayson and Rachel Stewart are confronted with dark details of Rachel's past. As more facts begin emerging, their new marriage is thrown into a tailspin. The newlyweds must figure out how to move forward . . . and Grayson must figure out if he married a killer.

## LANTERN BEACH BLACKOUT

**Dark Water**

Colton Locke can't forget the black op that went terribly wrong. Desperate for a new start, he moves to Lantern Beach, North Carolina, and forms Blackout, a private security firm. Despite his hero status, he can't erase the mistakes he's made. For the past year, Elise Oliver hasn't been able to shake the feeling that there's more to her husband's death than she was told. When she finds a hidden box of his personal possessions, more questions—and suspicions—arise. The only person she trusts to help her is her husband's best friend, Colton Locke. Someone wants Elise dead. Is it because she knows too much? Or is it to keep her from finding the truth? The Blackout team must uncover dark secrets hiding beneath seemingly still waters. But those very secrets might just tear the team apart.

**Safe Harbor**

Guilt over past mistakes haunts former Navy SEAL Dez Rodriguez. When he's asked to guard a pop star during a music festival on Lantern Beach, he's all set for what he hopes is a breezy assignment. Bree hasn't found fame to be nearly as fulfilling as she dreamed. Instead, she's more like a carefully crafted character living out a pre-scripted story. When a stalker's threats become deadly, her life—and career—are turned upside down. From the start, Bree sees her temporary bodyguard as a player, and Dez sees Bree as a spoiled rich girl. But when they're thrown together in a fight for survival, both must learn to trust. Can Dez protect Bree—and his carefully guarded heart? Or will their safe harbor ultimately become their death trap?

**Ripple Effect**

Griff McIntyre never expected his ex-wife and three-year-old daughter to come to Lantern Beach. After an abduction attempt, they're desperate for safety. Now Griff's not letting either of them out of his sight. Bethany knows Griff is the only one who can protect them, despite the fact that he broke her heart. But she'll do anything to keep her daughter safe—even if it means playing nicely with a man she can't stand. As peril ripples through their lives, Griff and Bethany must work together to protect their daughter. But an unseen enemy wants something from them . . . and will stop at nothing to get it. When disaster strikes, can Griff keep his family safe? Or will past mistakes bring the ultimate failure?

**Rising Tide**

Benjamin James knows there's a traitor within his former command. The rest of his team might even think it's him. As danger closes in, he must clear himself and stop a deadly plot by a dangerous terrorist group. All CJ Compton wanted was a new start after her career ended under suspicion. Working as the house manager for private security group

Blackout seems perfect. But there's more trouble here than what she left behind. As the tide rushes in, the stakes continue to rise. If the Blackout team fails, it's not just Lantern Beach at stake—it's the whole country. Can Benjamin and CJ overcome their differences and work together to find the truth?

## LANTERN BEACH GUARDIANS

### Hide and Seek

*During a turbulent storm, a child is found on the beach, washed up from the ocean. Making matters worse—the girl can't speak.* Lantern Beach Police Chief Cassidy Chambers can feel the danger lurking around them. As more mysterious incidents happen on the island, Cassidy fears each crime is somehow connected to this child—a child no one has reported missing. Cassidy knows the girl's life depends on finding answers. With the help of her husband, Ty, a former Navy SEAL, she scrambles to discover what exactly is going on. Someone appears to be playing a deadly version of hide-and-seek—and using the girl as a pawn. But what will happen when the game finally ends? *Hide and Seek is the first book in a three book series. Though the main storyline of each book will be wrapped up at the end, some plot lines will not be resolved until the end of book three.*

**Shock and Awe**

They thought the worst was over—but they were wrong.When Police Chief Cassidy Chambers arrives at a grisly crime scene, she's shocked at where the evidence leads. Then the threats start coming. Threats against her. Threats that could upend her life.As more clues are uncovered, a sinister plot is revealed, and Cassidy fears the little girl in her care may be tangled in a deadly scheme. Cassidy and her husband, Ty, will do anything to protect the child, each other, and the island. But what happens when they might not be able to save all three?

**Safe and Sound**

A call for help draws Police Chief Cassidy Chambers deep into a wooded, isolated area on Lantern Beach. What she finds shakes her to the core—a friend is bleeding out, and his last words before dying are: They know. Figuring out who killed her friend and what his final words meant becomes Cassidy's mission. Have members of the notorious gang that placed a bounty on her head discovered her new life? Or is someone else trying to teach her a twisted lesson? Elements from past investigations surface and threaten more than one person's safety. Cassidy and her husband, Ty, must make sense of the deadly secrets that unfold at every turn. If not, the life they've built together might come to a permanent end.

## LANTERN BEACH BLACKOUT: THE NEW RECRUITS

**Rocco**

Former Navy SEAL and new Blackout recruit Rocco Foster is on a simple in and out mission. But the operation turns complicated when an unsuspecting woman wanders into the line of fire. Peyton Ellison's life mission is to sprinkle happiness on those around her. When a cupcake delivery turns into a fight for survival, she must trust her rescuer—a handsome stranger—to keep her safe. Rocco is determined to figure out why someone is targeting Peyton. First, he must keep the intriguing woman safe and earn her trust. But threats continue to pummel them as incriminating evidence emerges and pits them against each other. With time running out, the two must set aside both their growing attraction and their doubts about each other in order to work together. But the perilous facts they discover leave them wondering what exactly the truth is . . . and if the truth can be trusted.

**Axel**

*Women are missing. Private security firm Blackout*

*must find them before another victim disappears.* Axel Hendrix likes to live on the edge. That's why being a Navy SEAL suited him so well. But after his last mission, he cut his losses and joined Blackout instead. His team's latest case involves an undercover investigation on Lantern Beach. Olivia Rollins came to the island to escape her problems—and danger. When trouble from her past shows up in town, she impulsively blurts she's engaged to Axel, the womanizing man she's seen while waitressing. Now, she may not be the only one in danger. So could Axel. Axel knows Olivia might be his chance to find answers and that acting like her fiancé is the perfect cover for his latest assignment. But he doesn't like throwing Olivia into the middle of such a dangerous situation. Nor is he comfortable with the feelings she stirs inside him. With Olivia's life—as well as both their hearts—on the line, Axel must uncover the truth and stop an evil plan before more lives are destroyed.

**Beckett**

*When the daughter of a federal judge is abducted, private security firm Blackout must find her.* Psychologist Samantha Reynolds doesn't know why someone is targeting her. Even after a risky mission to save her, danger still lingers. She's determined to use her insights into the human mind to help decode the deadly clues being left in the wake of her rescue. Former Navy SEAL Beckett Jones needs to figure out who's responsible for the crimes hounding Sami. He's not sure why he's so protective of the woman he rescued, but he'll do anything to keep her safe—even if it means risking his heart. As the body count rises, there's no room for error. Beckett and Sami must both tear down the careful walls they've built around themselves in order to survive. If they don't figure out who's responsible, the madman will continue his death spree . . . and one of them might be next.

**Gabe**

When former Navy SEAL and current Blackout operative Gabe Michaels is almost killed in a hit-and-run, the aftermath completely upends his life. He's no longer safe—and he's not the only one. Dr. Autumn Spenser came to Lantern Beach to start fresh. But while treating Gabe after his accident, she senses there's more to what happened to him than meets the eye. When she digs deeper into his past, she never expects to be drawn into a deadly dilemma. Gabe has been infatuated with the pretty doctor since the day they met. Now, can he keep her from harm? Could someone out of his league ever return his feelings or will her past hurts keep them apart? As danger continues to pummel them, Gabe and Autumn are thrown together in a quest to find answers. More important than their growing attraction, they must stay alive long enough to stop the person desperate to destroy them.

## LANTERN BEACH MAYDAY

### Run Aground

A dead captain on a luxury yacht leads to a tumultuous seafaring journey . . . Med student Kenzie Anderson, tired of letting others chart her future, accepts a job as second steward aboard Almost Paradise. But when she finds the captain dead before the charter even begins, her plans seem to capsize. Jimmy James Gamble senses something vulnerable and slightly naive about Kenzie when he finds her on the docks. Realizing danger may still be lingering close, he uses his hidden skills to earn a place on the charter. But being there causes him to risk everything—especially as more suspicious incidents occur. As they set out to sea, Kenzie and Jimmy James both wonder if they're in over their heads. They must figure out how to stop a killer before anyone onboard is hurt . . . otherwise, both their futures might just run aground.

### Dead Reckoning

A yachtie fears for her life when she's the only witness to a murder . . . Kenzie Anderson knows what she saw at the harbor—a woman strangled and pushed overboard. But there's no proof of a crime . . . only her word. Jimmy James Gamble believes Kenzie, even if no one else does. As he senses the danger in the air, all he wants is to keep her away from any more trouble—especially after their last charter. Either Kenzie or the yacht they're working on seem to be a magnet for murder and mayhem. Someone is willing to kill to get what he wants—and will do so again if necessary. Can Jimmy James and Kenzie navigate these unfamiliar waters? Or will relying on dead reckoning lead them to their deaths?

**Tipping Point**

Awakening in a boat surrounded by nothing but water, a yachtie has no doubt someone wants her dead. Kenzie Anderson is determined not to let anyone scare her away from completing the charter season—even with the threats on her life. The only person she can trust is Captain Jimmy James Gamble, despite their tumultuous relationship. Kenzie and Jimmy James both suspect turbulent currents rush beneath the tranquil surface aboard the luxury yacht Almost Paradise. Secrets seem to abound, each one increasing the tension aboard the boat. As answers rise to the surface, neither Kenzie nor Jimmy James is prepared for what they find. Have they both reached their tipping points? Their adversaries want nothing more than to make Kenzie disappear . . . forever. It may be too late for a mayday call.

## LANTERN BEACH CHRISTMAS

### Silent Night

Catch up with your favorite Lantern Beach characters as they come together to help the town's beloved police chief. On the night before Christmas Eve, as she begins her maternity leave, Lantern Beach Police Chief Cassidy Chambers disappears. Suspecting foul play, law enforcement officers combine forces with the Blackout Security team and island residents to find her. Despite a snowstorm in his path, Cassidy's husband, Ty, desperately tries to return home in time to save her. With his wife's and baby's lives on the line, he needs a Christmas miracle. Will the tightknit community of Lantern Beach be able to rescue their beloved police chief in time? Or will Cassidy's cries for help be met only with silence?

## LANTERN BEACH BLACKOUT: DANGER RISING

### Brandon

*Physically he's protecting her. But emotionally she's never felt more exposed.* The last person tech heiress Finley Cooper ever wanted to see again was Brandon

Hale. Two years ago, Brandon shattered her heart. Now Finley needs protection, and, against her wishes, Brandon is assigned the job. Even worse, they must pretend to be a couple in order to find answers. Brandon, a former Navy SEAL, met Finley while on an undercover assignment in Ecuador. But he broke her trust, and now he doesn't blame Finley for hating him. As a new Blackout operative, Brandon's first assignment throws him into Finley's life 24/7. Someone wants her dead, and it's clear this person won't stop until that mission is accomplished. To keep her safe, Brandon must regain Finley's trust. Can he convince her she's more than a job to him? Or will peril permanently silence them?

**Dylan**

*His job is to protect her. The trouble is . . . she doesn't want protection.* Former Navy SEAL Dylan Granger's new assignment requires him to use both his tactical abilities and his acting skills. Hired by Katie Logan's father, his job is to protect the gutsy university professor while concealing his identity. To maintain his cover, he takes the unassuming role of her new assistant. Katie—a disgraced reporter—has stumbled upon a lead she can't ignore. Now it's clear someone is targeting her, but she refuses to back down. Her handsome new assistant is a welcome distraction from the chaos. But Dylan's skillset goes way beyond his job description, and Katie begins to suspect there's more to Dylan than he's letting on. Dylan's mission can't be disclosed—not if he wants to keep Katie safe. But as his feelings for her grow and the danger increases, keeping his secret becomes more of a challenge than he ever imagined. With innocent lives on the line, Dylan must choose between protecting Katie or savings others.

**Maddox**

*He's on the case . . . and she's his prime suspect.* Classified technology is missing, a delivery driver is dead, and former Navy SEAL Maddox King must find the culprits before a dangerous plan is enacted. To find answers, the Blackout agent must go undercover as a maintenance man at millionaire Seymore Whitlock's estate. While there, he sets his sights on Whitlock's personal assistant, Taryn Parsons, a woman who has everything to gain and nothing to lose. Six months ago, Whitlock plucked Taryn out of obscurity to become his caretaker. But with deadly incidents haunting the estate, Taryn doesn't know who she can trust—including the new maintenance man who is both intriguing . . . and unnerving. The stakes continue to escalate, and Maddox is running out of time to find answers. With the body count rising along with his list of suspects, this assignment may be his most challenging yet . . . for both his skillset and his heart.

**Titus**

She shattered his heart once. Can he set her betrayal aside for the sake of his country? The last person Titus Armstrong wants to join forces with is the woman who dumped him for his brother, Alex. But Presley Lennox is Blackout's best chance at infiltrating a dangerous organization known as The System and finding out more about their deadly plans. Presley Lennox wants out—of both an abusive relationship and the radical group she's become entangled with because of Alex. When Titus reappears in her life, he's like an answer to prayer—until he asks her to dive deeper into the very life she's been trying to escape. A dangerous plan is brewing that could destroy thousands of lives. Titus and Presley may be the only ones who can stop what's about to be unleashed. Failure would mean certain chaos . . . not only for them but for their nation.

## BEACH BOUND BOOKS AND BEANS MYSTERIES

**Bound by Murder**

When widow Talitha Robinson buys an old store on the boardwalk in Lantern Beach, North Carolina, she's in for a surprise . . . or several. She plans to renovate the space and open Beach Bound Books and Beans, but never expects to find a decades-old skeleton hidden inside one of the walls. As word of the discovery spreads across the island, strange occurrences begin to occur around her. It soon becomes clear someone still knows something about the dead person—something they don't want discovered. Thankfully, former police chief and current mayor Mac MacArthur seems just as eager to unravel the mystery behind the skeletal remains as Tali. But as the two bind together to solve the case, a devastating secret is revealed. Will their newfound friendship come unglued before they find the answers to the past? Or will their blooming relationship die like the man hidden in the wall?Bound by Murder is book 1 in a four book series of novellas. Though the main mystery is resolved, there are threads that will continue throughout the entire series.

**Bound by Disaster**

Talitha Robinson is knee-deep in renovations as she prepares to open her new bookstore when a body washes ashore on Lantern Beach. While news of the suspicious death surges across the island, a stranger comes knocking on Tali's door, begging her to endorse his unfinished suspense novel. Unable to dissuade the author, Tali is left holding his manuscript in her hands. But she has no idea of the peril written on its pages. Mac MacArthur has kept his distance from Tali since they uncovered a shocking connection about their pasts. But when someone begins to act out the murderous scenes from the book, one victim at a time, Mac's protective instincts override his decision to stay away. As danger escalates, Mac and Tali must manage their conflicting feelings as they work together to stop this killer . . . before the last chapter is written.

**Bound by Mystery**

Talitha Robinson is well on her way to completing renovations for her new bookstore, Beach Bound Books and Beans, in Lantern Beach, North Carolina. But when she hosts a friendly meet-and-greet with bookstore owners from nearby islands, the progress she's making comes to a deadly end. Someone is backstabbed—literally—right under Tali's nose. To make matters worse, Tali's fingerprints are all over the murder weapon and a neighbor claims to have seen Tali commit the crime. Mac MacArthur knows Tali isn't the type to hurt anyone, but it doesn't take a former police chief to figure out things don't look good for her. The two work together to read between the lines and decipher the truth before Tali gets locked away for crimes she didn't commit. As more evidence stacks up, it becomes clear that someone wants to take Tali out of the story. For good.

**Bound by Trouble**

With the grand opening of Beach Bound Books and Beans, Tali Robinson's dreams are finally coming true. She hopes to now put the past behind her and start a new chapter. When a suspicious stranger mysteriously shows up at her celebration, her hopes disappear faster than a bestseller at a book signing.Mac MacArthur is ready to solidify his relationship with Tali. But mending their differences is easier said than done. Then someone sets their sights on Tali—and wants to put her out of print . . . permanently. With trouble brewing, Tali and Mac have no choice but to dive into the chaos of the past. However, as more answers are revealed, the danger increases. The truth will come at a great cost . . . one that will bind them together or drive them apart.

**Bound by Mayhem**

As cast and crew members prepare for Lantern Beach's first annual Christmas play, catastrophe strikes. Abby Mendez, the director and brainchild behind the play, never shows up for a dress rehearsal. Threats emerge, and it becomes clear that not everyone on the island feels the Christmas spirit. With dangerous encounters and ghostly disappearing acts threatening not only the play but also the safety of Lantern Beach residents, former police chief Mac MacArthur and Abby's friend Tali Robinson jump in to help. The stakes rise as the perpetrator continues to haunt Abby's past, torment her present, and threaten her future. When it seems all hope is nearly lost, can the people of Lantern Beach work together to save the play? Or will this phantom scrooge steal the final act?

# ABOUT THE AUTHOR

*USA Today* has called Christy Barritt's books "scary, funny, passionate, and quirky."

Christy writes both mystery and romantic suspense novels that are clean with underlying messages of faith. Her books have sold more than four million copies and have won the Daphne du Maurier Award for Excellence in Suspense and Mystery, have been twice nominated for the Romantic Times Reviewers' Choice Award, and have finaled for both a Carol Award and Foreword Magazine's Book of the Year.

She is married to her Prince Charming, a man who thinks she's hilarious—but only when she's not trying to be. Christy is a self-proclaimed klutz, an avid music lover who's known for spontaneously bursting into song, and a road trip aficionado.

When she's not working or spending time with her family, she enjoys singing, playing the guitar, and exploring small, unsuspecting towns where people have no idea how accident-prone she is.

Find Christy online at:
**www.christybarritt.com**
**www.facebook.com/christybarritt**
**www.twitter.com/cbarritt**

Sign up for Christy's newsletter to get information on all of her latest releases here: **www.christybarritt.com/newsletter-sign-up/**

facebook.com / AuthorChristyBarritt
twitter.com / christybarritt
instagram.com / cebarritt